The Mystery of ⌐

A Story for Bo

George Barton

Alpha Editions

This edition published in 2024

ISBN : 9789361479816

Design and Setting By
Alpha Editions
www.alphaedis.com
Email - info@alphaedis.com

Contents

CHAPTER I IN WHICH A BULLY COMES TO GRIEF ....- 1 -

CHAPTER II HERBERT FINDS HIMSELF THE INNOCENT CAUSE OF MUCH TROUBLE ....-4 -

CHAPTER III PROVING THAT BIRDS OF A FEATHER FLOCK TOGETHER ....- 10 -

CHAPTER IV IN WHICH FORTUNE UNEXPECTEDLY FAVORS DAVID HARKINS ....- 15 -

CHAPTER V IN WHICH DAVID HARKINS BECOMES THE VICTIM OF PECULIAR CIRCUMSTANCES ....- 18 -

CHAPTER VI IN WHICH DAVID HARKINS QUITS THIS LIFE AND TAKES HIS SECRET WITH HIM ....- 23 -

CHAPTER VII IN WHICH HERBERT MEETS ADVERSITY AND LEARNS THE MEANING OF HARD WORK ....- 28 -

CHAPTER VIII HERBERT BECOMES AMBITIOUS AND IS FASCINATED BY THE SMELL OF PRINTERS' INK ....- 32 -

CHAPTER IX HAVING BECOME A NEWSPAPER WRITER, HERBERT LOOKS FOR NEW WORLDS TO CONQUER...- 38 -

CHAPTER X WHICH TELLS OF HOW HERBERT CAME TO LEAVE THE TOWN OF CLEVERLY ....- 44 -

CHAPTER XI HERBERT IS AWED AND AMAZED BY HIS FIRST SIGHT OF A GREAT CITY ....- 49 -

CHAPTER XII IN WHICH HERBERT BECOMES ACQUAINTED WITH SOME OF THE METHODS OF MODERN JOURNALISM ....- 55 -

CHAPTER XIII HERBERT MAKES A HIT AND TIDES OVER A TEMPORARY FINANCIAL DIFFICULTY ....- 61 -

CHAPTER XIV IN WHICH HERBERT IS GIVEN AN UNUSUAL OPPORTUNITY TO DISTINGUISH HIMSELF - 65 -

CHAPTER XV IN WHICH HERBERT DOES SOME VERY HARD WORK AND RECEIVES A TERRIBLE SHOCK.......- 69 -

CHAPTER XVI IN WHICH HERBERT LOSES HIS POSITION AND RETIRES IN DISGRACE ....- 73 -

CHAPTER XVII THE YOUNG REPORTER FINDS THAT THE DOOR OF OPPORTUNITY IS BARRED TO HIM........- 78 -

CHAPTER XVIII WHEREIN A BLACK SHEEP SHOWS A DESIRE TO CHANGE HIS COLOR....................................- 82 -

CHAPTER XIX PERSISTENCE HAS ITS REWARD AND HERBERT FINALLY MEETS THE MYSTERIOUS STRANGER ....- 86 -

CHAPTER XX IN WHICH A STAIN IS REMOVED FROM THE MEMORY OF AN INNOCENT MAN................- 92 -

CHAPTER XXI IN WHICH A TELEPHONE CALL PRODUCES SOME UNEXPECTED RESULTS ....- 96 -

CHAPTER XXII PROVING THAT BAD PERSONS, LIKE BAD PENNIES, ARE CONSTANTLY REAPPEARING ....- 100 -

CHAPTER XXIII IN WHICH A BAD MAN REACHES THE END OF HIS ROPE..- 105 -

CHAPTER XXIV WHEREIN THE CLOUDS PASS AWAY AND THE SUN SHINES ON HERBERT HARKINS ....- 110 -

CHAPTER XXV DEMONSTRATING THE TRUTH OF THE SAYING THAT ALL'S WELL THAT ENDS WELL ....- 116 -

CHAPTER I
IN WHICH A BULLY COMES TO GRIEF

"If you fellows don't open that door and let me in, there'll be trouble in this town before long."

The only answer was a mocking laugh from the group of boys to whom this threat was addressed.

Herbert Harkins, his face red with rage, pounded his fist on the panels of the schoolhouse without making the slightest impression upon his fellow schoolboys.

"Open the door," he cried again, in a loud voice.

Once more a peal of laughter sounded from within. The scene of this incident was the Cleverly District School. The time was the second of January, and the occasion was the annual frolic of the boys, known as "barring out day."

It was a custom which, originating down east, had spread to the little town in New Jersey. The method was quite simple. After the Christmas holidays the big boys put their heads together and decided on a plan of campaign. When all of the details had been arranged, it was decided to put them into execution at the first regular session of the new year. The forenoon passed off as quietly as any other day, the boys looking very sober and extremely attentive to their studies, and keeping unusual order. The moment the schoolmaster left the house for his dinner and the smaller children were started homeward, the doors and windows were suddenly and securely locked, and the older pupils proceeded to spend the afternoon in play and hilarity.

When Mr. Anderson, the teacher, returned about one o'clock, he was surprised to find the schoolhouse in a state of siege. He made an attempt to enter, but failed. It so happened that Herbert Harkins was the only one of the larger boys who had been locked out. Under ordinary circumstances he would have taken the incident good-naturedly; but in this case he knew that the teacher was frail and delicate, and Herbert's regard and sympathy for Mr. Anderson aroused all his manly instincts and brought his fighting blood to the boiling pitch. The teacher who had been employed in this district only a few weeks, was evidently of a sickly disposition. It was a cold day. He was insufficiently clad, and the prospect of taking some sickness which might perhaps lead to pneumonia and death made the poor man quite miserable. His face was beginning to get blue with the intense cold; but he was too weak to resort to any physical methods for opening the door.

Herbert knocked again; but his appeal was received only with jeers and shouts of derision. Mr. Anderson turned to him with a kindly smile, and said:

"There is no need of doing anything more, Herbert. I thank you for your good intentions; but I think the only thing left for me to do is to go home for the day."

As Herbert was about to reply he happened to glance upward and noticed the smoke coming from the chimney on the top of the schoolhouse. He remembered that the room was heated by means of an old-fashioned wood fire, which was constantly replenished during the day. Whenever a fresh or green log was placed on the fire, more or less smoke went up the chimney. As Herbert gazed at the little curls of smoke making their way skyward, he suddenly conceived a means of breaking up the siege in the schoolhouse and procuring entrance for himself and the teacher. To think was to act. A small pile of lumber lay in the roadway nearby. Herbert walked over to it and picked out a wide, square board. It was quite heavy; but by dint of much energy and persistence he managed to get it under his arm and carry it to the schoolhouse. Mr. Anderson wondered what he was about to do. The boys on the inside, too, gazed at this unexpected activity with much interest. Herbert's next move was to secure a large ladder, which he put up against the side of the house. Then reaching for the board, he made his way to the top of the schoolhouse and in less than two minutes had placed it over the top of the chimney. Then he hurried down the ladder again, and rejoining Mr. Anderson, said calmly:

"I am willing to wager that we will be inside of that schoolroom before you have time to count a hundred."

And so it proved. The smoke, unable to find its way out of the chimney, was thrown back into the schoolroom, and in a minute's time the boys were choking from the effects of the fumes. Some were in favor of holding out, but when their eyes began to run water and they were filled with a stifling sensation, they quickly decided to surrender. The bars were taken down and the doors and windows thrown open.

Herbert, delighted with the success of his little scheme, remounted the ladder, and going to the roof, took the board from the chimney. The boys made no further attempts at disturbance; within fifteen minutes order had been entirely restored, and the afternoon session went on as if nothing had happened.

Most of the boys were filled with admiration at Herbert's cleverness; but a few of them murmured against him and threatened to punish him for breaking up their fun. The largest of these boys was Arthur Black, who was a year older than Herbert, and had the reputation of being the bully of the school. After the children had been dismissed for the afternoon, they gathered in groups outside the schoolhouse and talked about the unusual event. Arthur Black raised his voice above the others, declaring that he had a great notion to thrash the boy who had dared to interfere with their sport. Some of the more timid pupils approached Herbert and advised him to hurry home in order to escape punishment. He smiled at their fears, however, and said he had no reason for running away. Just then Arthur Black approached.

"What's that you say?" he asked in an insulting voice.

"I said that I had no reason for running away," replied Herbert quietly.

"Well, that's because you haven't got any sense," was the ugly rejoinder. "You're a sneak and a busybody and ought to be thrown out of the school."

"Why?" asked Herbert.

"Because you spoiled our fun," was the reply.

"I don't think it's much fun to keep a sick teacher out in the cold and make him run the risk of losing his life. I—"

"Oh, we've had enough of your talk," said Arthur, interrupting Herbert.

"But you will listen to what I have to say," persisted Herbert manfully.

"No I won't," was the rejoinder, "and if you say another word I'll thrash you within an inch of your life."

"Two can play at that game," said Herbert coolly.

The other made no reply, but began to take off his coat, and flinging it on the ground, started to roll up his shirt sleeves. Instantly the other boys formed a ring about them. There was nothing left for Herbert but to accept the invitation that was thrown down to him in such a noisy way. He took off his coat, and in a trice the two boys were engaged in a rough and tumble fight. It looked for a time as if Arthur Black, who was the older and heavier of the two, would get the better of Herbert. The boys crowded around the two fighters and urged them on with yells and shouts of approval. Herbert kept comparatively cool, and at a critical stage in the fight he pummeled Arthur so vigorously that he cried for mercy. Indeed his nose was bleeding and one of his eyes was beginning to show evidence of the contest. Picking up his hat and coat, and hardly able to repress his tears, he hurried off towards his home. Herbert was immediately proclaimed the hero of the hour. He had thrashed the bully of the school, and from that moment he was the idol of his schoolmates and the most popular boy in Cleverly.

CHAPTER II
HERBERT FINDS HIMSELF THE INNOCENT CAUSE OF MUCH TROUBLE

When Herbert Harkins reached home he found that the story of his battle with Arthur Black had preceded him. His mother was at the doorway awaiting his arrival. She scanned his face anxiously.

"Are you hurt, Herbert?" she asked.

"Not a great deal, mother," he said, with a trace of conscious pride in his voice; "but I can't say as much for the other fellow."

"I was sorry to hear that you were quarreling," she remarked gravely; "it's not gentlemanly."

"But I could not let the other boys think I was a coward," he cried quickly.

His mother made no reply to this, but pointing toward the sitting room, said simply:

"Your father is waiting to see you."

Herbert started up the stairway, filled with misgivings. It was a rare thing for his father to send for him, and the serious manner in which his mother had delivered the message convinced him that it must be a matter of importance. David Harkins was above everything else a just man. He had started out in life with bright prospects, but through a series of misfortunes over which he had no control, his little fortune had been very much reduced and his health greatly impaired.

His doctor advised him to go into the country and engage in open air work as much as possible. He cautioned him above all else to avoid the occasions of excitement. The medical man assured him that his heart was weak, and that it would not stand any severe or unusual strain. Mr. Harkins examined various properties in the vicinity of the city, and finally decided upon the neat little place at Cleverly. It contained a garden and was within a reasonable distance of the city whence Mr. Harkins' employment called him several times a week. In the meantime he cultivated the garden, and by dint of close economy managed to make both ends meet. Mr. Harkins was engaged in looking over some papers when Herbert entered the room. He laid them down immediately and turned to the boy with a look in which affection and reproach were mingled.

"Herbert, I hear bad reports about you."

"I'm sorry for that, father," was the response, "because I don't believe I deserve them."

Mr. Harkins glanced at Herbert keenly, and the look which he received in return seemed to satisfy him, for he said:

"Tell me in your own way all about this quarrel—give me all the details, and do not attempt to hide anything."

Herbert told everything clearly and quickly. As he concluded his father nodded his head as if to indicate that he understood and then sighed deeply. Herbert noticed this, and said with trembling voice:

"You believe me, don't you?"

"I do."

"Don't you think I did right?"

"I do."

"But why are you so sad?"

"Because I regret this thing very much—because I am sorry you quarreled with Arthur Black."

"But you said I was justified."

"I did; but unfortunately you have offended a powerful man. I suppose you are old enough to understand these things. John Black, Arthur's father, is not only the richest man in Cleverly, but he is the president of the bank, and I— I owe him money."

David Harkins put his head in his hands as he spoke, and leaning on his desk, sat there for some time buried in thought. Herbert was silent for awhile, then rushing up to his father, cried out impulsively:

"I'm awfully sorry, father; I didn't intend to do anything wrong. I never thought of injuring you. If I can repair the damage in any way I'll be only too glad to do so. Tell me what to do."

"Do," cried his father, with a sudden return of his natural dignity; "why do nothing; you are guilty of no wrong and have nothing to regret. However," with a sigh which he could not conceal, "I'm sure we will hear more about this before the evening is over."

And so they did. About eight o'clock that night there was a loud rapping at the door, and a stout, pompous man was ushered into the parlor. He had iron gray hair, heavy bristling eyebrows and scowled in the most severe manner. He looked about the little room in a disdainful manner, and then dropped abruptly into the easiest chair at hand. His manner was aggressive.

He carried a heavy cane and pounded it on the floor impatiently while awaiting the arrival of Mr. Harkins.

Such was John Black, bank president, capitalist and the most unpopular man in Cleverly.

"See here, Harkins," he cried out abruptly as Herbert's father entered the room, "I came to see you about that boy of yours."

"What about him?" asked Mr. Harkins quietly.

"A great deal about him," spluttered the banker, "he's a young rowdy; that's what he is. He set on my boy Arthur at school to-day and beat him in the most brutal manner."

"A boys' fight?" queried Herbert's father lifting his eyebrows.

"You may call it a boys' fight," thundered the other; "I call it an outrage. Why that child of mine came home with his nose bleeding—do you understand sir—with his nose bleeding."

"That child as you call him," ventured Mr. Harkins, a note of amusement in his voice, "is, I believe, nearly seventeen years old."

"What's that got to do with it?" shouted the other.

"Nothing, except that he's nearly two years older than my boy."

"Age is not the only thing—"

"No," interrupted Mr. Harkins, "weight should be considered. Arthur is not only older, but he is much heavier than Herbert."

"Do you mean to say," exclaimed the banker in amazement, "that you are taking up for that boy?"

"Oh, no," said Mr. Harkins pleasantly, "that's not necessary. Herbert seems to be fully capable of taking up for himself."

"Take care, Harkins," said the rich man, banging his cane angrily on the floor; "take care; don't attempt to trifle with me!"

David Harkins paid no attention to this outburst, but sat silent wondering what would come next. His curiosity was soon satisfied.

John Black arose with a gesture of impatience.

"There is no need of my wasting any more time here," he exclaimed. "I came over to give you a chance to set yourself straight."

"To set myself straight?" queried Harkins.

"Yes; if you have that boy of yours apologize to Arthur at school to-morrow, we'll call it quits."

David Harkins stood looking at the banker as if he had taken leave of his senses. The silence lasted so long that it became embarrassing.

"Come, come, what do you say to my proposal?" asked John Black. "I don't want to be too hard on your young one. Do as I say and the matter will drop. Your answer."

"No!" shouted Harkins. "No; a hundred times no! Herbert did perfectly right in thrashing that bully of a son of yours. I'm proud of him for doing it. And if he would dare to apologize for it I'd disown him as a son."

John Black grew almost livid with rage. He hurried to the door. When he reached it he looked back and shook his cane at Harkins.

"You will regret this insult; blast you, I'll make you sorry for what you said."

Mrs. Harkins entered the room just as the banker retired. She hurried over to her husband.

"I heard loud voices, David," she said. "I am sorry you quarreled with Mr. Black."

Her husband looked at her fondly. His face was pale, although he was smiling.

"I'm sorry, too," he said; "but he irritated me beyond endurance. Besides I told him the truth. Between ourselves," he added, "I'm really proud of Herbert."

"But you must not tell that to Herbert," she said anxiously; "it might be the means of spoiling him."

"Oh, never fear, I won't tell him; but I won't be unjust to the boy either. I'll deal fairly with him."

Indeed, as has already been indicated, a love of justice was one of the most striking traits of David Harkins' character, and unconsciously he was doing all in his power to plant the same virtue in the mind and heart of his only son.

"In spite of what you say, David," remarked Mrs. Harkins, "I regret this incident. I do not believe in signs or any nonsense of that sort, but some strange voice within me says that this thing will have a fatal ending."

"Oh, cheer up," was the bright response of the husband. "It's folly to look on the dark side of life. Anyhow, what will be, must be. All that we can do in this life is to try and live decently. A friend of mine used to say that it was a good thing always to hope for the best and prepare for the worst."

With this bit of philosophy Mr. Harkins turned to his desk and resumed his work. As his wife closed the door, however, the cheerful look left his face, and lines of care and worry began to appear. Despite his protests to the contrary, he regretted his encounter with John Black. But his sense of right and justice was too acute to permit him to make peace at the price of truth.

While he was thinking over the events of the day, there was a ring of the door-bell, and in a moment Mrs. Harkins appeared to present Mr. Horace Coke, the lawyer of Cleverly and one of the good friends of the family. Mr. Coke was one of the old fashioned attorneys at law. He wore a suit of black broadcloth and carried a cane and a high silk hat in his hand. He had a smooth, round face, was always in a good humor, loved children and dogs, and lived in constant peace and harmony with his friends and neighbors.

Mr. Harkins hastened to give him the most comfortable chair in the room, and Mrs. Harkins, who had remained, waited expectantly to hear the occasion of the visit. The visitor stroked his chin in an absent-minded way and seemed ill at ease. He was not smiling either, which was a strange thing for Horace Coke. Presently he said abruptly:

"It's a lovely evening Dave, isn't it?"

"Yes," replied Mr. Harkins, "it is a lovely evening."

But he knew in his heart that the lawyer had not called to make this useless comment on the weather. He knew that something more important was to come, so he sat silent and waited.

"Dave," said the lawyer, clearing his throat, "I'm here on a very, very unpleasant errand. It was in the line of my professional duty though, and I couldn't get out of it."

"Indeed," was the non-committal reply.

"No," pursued Mr. Coke, "you see I am here representing a client."

"Might I ask the name of your client?"

"Yes; it is John Black."

Mr. Harkins started as he heard this name. It was not altogether unexpected, yet the sound gave him an uncomfortable feeling. Mrs. Harkins, too, was very much depressed by the announcement. Herbert had entered the room quietly during the conversation; but when he heard what Mr. Coke had said, he paused at the threshold.

"Well," said Mr. Harkins finally, "what about Mr. Black?"

"It seems," replied the lawyer, "that you have had a financial transaction with Mr. Black."

"Yes, sir."

"That he has your note for one thousand dollars."

"That is correct."

"Well, Mr. Black sends me here to collect it."

"Mr. Coke, isn't this a rather unusual method of doing business? I borrowed this money from Mr. Black at the bank to pay off the mortgage on my house. I understood that it was to run for several years, although we had no written agreement regarding the time. But I never heard of a banker sending a lawyer to collect a note."

"It is unusual," confessed the lawyer, "but Mr. Black has the legal right to do it if he sees fit. He says the endorsers of the note are no good and he instructs me, if payment is not made within twenty-four hours, to proceed against you."

He arose to go. As he reached the door he turned and said:

"Dave, I don't think this is a square deal; but I'm only acting as a lawyer for a client. If I had the money to spare, I'd give it to you myself."

He said good-night and departed. Mrs. Harkins turned to her husband.

"Can you meet this demand, Dave?"

He looked at her in a strained sort of way. It was a half minute before he spoke. He said simply:

"I haven't the faintest idea where I am going to get the money."

CHAPTER III
PROVING THAT BIRDS OF A FEATHER FLOCK TOGETHER

Herbert was deeply impressed with the scene that had taken place between his father and Mr. Coke. It was quite early in the evening, and putting on his hat and coat, he quietly left the house for the purpose of taking a walk around the town and thinking over the meaning of the events which were following each other so quickly. He was filled with remorse at the thought of having been the innocent cause of bringing disaster on their modest household; but deep down in his heart he felt that he had done the right thing in spite of the unexpected results that had followed. Herbert had always been a sturdy and resolute boy.

He had regard for the feelings and rights of others, but was always quick to resent any attempt to impose upon his own good nature. When he first entered the school at Cleverly he did not give promise of being a very bright pupil. In fact there were times when the teacher was disposed to consider him a very dull boy; but little by little the ability that slumbered with him was awakened, and by degrees he began to show evidences of more than ordinary talent. He was not quick to learn; but was always numbered among the plodders at the school. In spite of his apparent slowness, he began to advance in his classes, and when he had reached his sixteenth year was near the head of the boys in his grade. For one thing he retained the knowledge that he acquired with so much labor. He had what the teacher called bull-dog tenacity. In other words, when he started out to accomplish a certain task he never rested till it was entirely completed.

Mr. Harkins, who was a man of very unusual ability, was extremely anxious to give his son the very best education in his power. His ambition was to develop Herbert both morally and mentally, and he looked forward with great hope to the time when he would finish his tuition at the Cleverly district school. After that it was his wish that he should enter St. Joseph's College in the adjoining city, in order to obtain a higher education. The Jesuits who were in charge of that institution, had offered four free scholarships to the boys who obtained the highest average in a competitive examination that was to be held in the spring of the year. The father and son had frequently discussed this subject.

"Herbert," said Mr. Harkins, "this is no child's play. If you make up your mind to go into this thing, it will mean hard work. There will be very little time for sports."

"I appreciate that, father," Herbert would say soberly. "And when the time comes I intend to pin myself down to the hardest kind of work. I know what it means, and I have no fear of the result."

So it was that the boy trudged along in his somewhat heavy way, doing the routine that fell to all the pupils of the Cleverly School. While he did not display any special flashes of brilliancy, his averages were always good, and sometimes unusually large.

Arthur Black was the opposite of Herbert in almost every way. For years he had been one of the favored pupils at the Cleverly School. The fact that his father was rich and influential made all those connected with the school disposed to treat him with more than ordinary consideration. He was a bright boy, but extremely indolent; and as a consequence was a source of constant trouble to his teachers. Arthur had the faculty of being able to recite his lessons without having given much time to their study; but as the weeks and months went by he became more and more indifferent and finally drifted down near the rear of his class where he bid fair to remain until the end of his school days. Arthur was very much annoyed at the progress made by Herbert Harkins, and publicly said that it was due to the fact that Herbert was one of the teacher's favorites. No charge could be more unfair than this, but it was circulated through the town, much to the annoyance of Herbert and his parents.

Herbert thought of all these things as he made his way along the main street of the town. He was filled with an intense desire to assist his father, and in a vague sort of way wondered whether it would not be a good thing to leave school and go to work for that purpose. The thought was worth considering anyhow, and he made up his mind to speak to his father before he left home the next morning. Just as he reached the post office pavement, he noticed a small group of men and boys standing there engaged in an animated discussion. As he approached nearer, he saw Arthur Black and a friend of his named Harry Adler talking for the benefit of the crowd. Adler was many years the senior of both Herbert and Arthur. He had the reputation of being a very worthless boy, and although he was rapidly approaching manhood he gave no indication of changing his habits. He was a type of many other boys who can be described in a single sentence as cigarette smoking youths who will not work. He said on one occasion that he was too proud to do menial labor, but in spite of this he was not ashamed to live off the small earnings of a poor mother who was compelled to take in sewing in order to feed and clothe the members of her family. Adler had persistently refused to go to school, and only two years before had run away from home and made his way by degrees to New York City. He remained there for several weeks, and then wrote begging letters home asking for sufficient money to pay his carfare back to Cleverly. He did not even have the manliness to be ashamed of this incident, but looked upon it as one of the big achievements in his life. Ever after that he stood on the street corners and talked in a loud way about his adventures in the big city, much to the amazement and interest of the small boys who stood with open mouths and eagerly listened to all that he had to say.

As Herbert reached the group he heard Arthur Black detailing the story of the fight at the schoolhouse. He informed his hearers that Herbert was a sneaking busybody, and that after school was over he had given him the punishment he so richly deserved.

"But when my back was turned," he said, "that rascal of a Herbert Harkins gave me a blow in the face that made my nose bleed. He wouldn't dare to have done it if we had been standing face to face."

This was too much for Herbert to stand, and turning toward the crowd with flashing eyes, he cried out:

"The story that Arthur Black has told you isn't true. He was the one at fault, and as far as the fight was concerned I think his nose and the color of his eyes tell the story of the battle better than I can."

Adler interrupted Herbert at this point to say in a sneering tone:

"See here, young man, if it comes to a question of truth between you and Arthur Black, the people of this town will believe Arthur."

"I don't know about that," retorted Herbert angrily. "Anyhow I would be willing to leave it to the people that know us both."

The minute Herbert had spoken he was sorry that his impulsive nature had led him into the conversation. In order to avoid any further trouble he hurried away; but Arthur Black and Harry Adler did not propose to let him off so easily.

"Hello there, little boy," cried Adler in a taunting voice. "Are you going to run away again, just as you did this afternoon?"

Herbert made no reply, but kept on his way. Then Arthur Black joined in the conversation.

"He'd better run away," he said, "if he knows which side his bread is buttered on. I want to tell you, Herbert Harkins, that you are going to suffer for daring to insult me. You say you won the fight this afternoon. Well, if you did, it will be the dearest victory you ever bought. Before another day goes by you will find that your whole family is likely to be thrown out into the street, and that you will be on your way to the poorhouse, where you belong. Perhaps you won't be so ready to meddle next time."

Herbert halted instantly. He hurried back to where the others were standing and made towards Arthur Black. Just as he passed by, Adler quietly slipped his right foot out on the sidewalk, and Herbert tripping over it, fell at full length on the pavement. He jumped up smarting with anger and the shock of the fall. He rushed toward Adler, but in the twinkling of an eye, before a blow had been struck, his mind reverted to the scene that had taken place at his home only a short while before. Instantly he was filled with remorse. He realized that it would be most unfortunate for him to get into a street brawl at a time like this. He felt confident of his ability to chastise both Arthur Black and Harry Adler; but he realized the scene that it would cause and the possibility of one or all of them being taken up by the town constable; so without any explanation whatever he lowered his arms and walked down the street again.

Adler turned to Arthur Black with a sneer on his lips.

"I guess you've got that fellow sized up all right," he said. "He's a coward; he's afraid to fight."

Herbert heard this with burning cheeks. He hurried on his way home, stopping to look neither to the right nor to the left. His mind was filled with conflicting emotions. He thought of the threat that hung over his father, and of the reflection that had been made upon his own personal courage; but try as he would he could not get the sound of that word "coward" out of his ears.

When he reached home the sense of shame had grown so strong that he could not stand the strain any longer. He halted on the doorstep irresolute. The next moment he turned on his heel and walked back to the corner where he had met Arthur Black and Harry Adler. Black had left, but Adler was still there entertaining some of the smaller boys with stories of his own greatness. Herbert walked up to him with flashing eyes:

"Adler, I've got a crow to pick with you."

"Go ahead with the picking," sneered the older boy, and Herbert flushed hotly at the contemptuous tone.

"A few minutes ago you referred to me as a coward."

"Well, what of it?"

"I want you to take that word back; I won't stand for it."

Adler broke out into a coarse laugh.

"Why, the little fellow is feeling his oats," he cried; "he looks like a bantam rooster."

"Never mind what I look like," retorted Herbert hotly. "I want to know whether you'll take that word back."

"Don't get excited, little chap."

"Will you take it back? Say yes or no!" demanded Herbert.

"I say no," drawled Adler.

"Then I say take that!"

As he spoke, Herbert reached up and gave the fellow a resounding slap on the cheek. Adler was so dazed at the unexpected assault that he stood still gazing stupidly at his assailant. The small boys in the group were secretly delighted at the indignity put upon their worthless companion, but were discreetly silent. Herbert walked off tingling with delight at having satisfied his outraged feelings.

CHAPTER IV
IN WHICH FORTUNE UNEXPECTEDLY FAVORS DAVID HARKINS

Herbert Harkins prepared to go to bed that night with a very heavy heart. He could not rid himself of the notion that he was the cause of the troubles that were gathering so rapidly about their home. Sleep is said to be the best medicine for a troubled mind; but unfortunately Herbert was not able to go to sleep. Usually he was in the land of dreams as soon as his head touched the pillow, but this night he was afflicted with a peculiar nervousness that could not be overcome. More than this he was greatly disturbed over the agitated condition of his father. He knew that he was sitting at his desk in the front room downstairs. He had spoken to him when he came home, and now from the light that was shining up the stairway he knew that his father was still awake. Presently he heard the movement of a chair, and then the steady tramping of feet indicating that Mr. Harkins was walking up and down the room.

Suddenly this monotonous sound was broken by a sharp rap on the front door. Herbert heard his father respond to the summons. The bolt was drawn back, the door opened, and then came a sound like the cry of recognition from two men. The door was softly closed again, and then came the steady mumbling of voices. This continued so long that Herbert became frightened. He got out of bed in the dark, and going into the hallway crept downstairs silently, step by step, until he had reached the doorway leading into the parlor. The light was turned down and the room was quite dim; but he could see his father and another man seated at a table engaged in earnest conversation. The stranger wore a full beard, and his head was covered with a great shock of red hair, in much disorder. The two men were so much engaged that they did not notice the half frightened boy standing near the doorway. Herbert on his part was so much interested in what he saw that for the time being he forgot the situation in which he had placed himself.

At times the two men were so close together that it would hardly have been possible to have drawn a sheet of paper between them. The stranger, in order to illustrate some point that he was making in his talk, threw his arm violently in the air, and in doing so overturned a little China ornament that was on the table, sending it crashing to the floor. Both men started violently at this unexpected happening, and then glanced nervously around the room as if to see whether anyone were listening. At the first sound of the falling ornament, Herbert started to run upstairs; but when the conversation was resumed some strange power seemed to draw him back to the doorway again. His intention was to take one last look and go away. He knew that he had no right there, and that his father might be very angry if he thought that he was out of bed and listening to the conversation; but some strange will over which he appeared to be powerless, kept him rooted to the spot. The two men talked in such a low tone at first that all he could hear was the mumbling of voices. Presently, however, his father becoming more earnest, said excitedly to the other man in a louder voice:

"I won't do it. I tell you I can't do it. It's not right to you."

"Don't be a fool," responded the red-haired man in a deep bass voice. "This will save you, and it cannot do me any harm. I'll never miss it, I can assure you."

"But it seems so unjust," urged his father; "it doesn't seem quite square to act with you in this way. After all these years I should not be placed in the position of taking this from you."

"I am the best judge of that," growled the other man in his heavy voice; "take it and say no more about it."

As he spoke he pushed a package in the direction of Mr. Harkins, who still with reluctance, picked it up and placed it in his pocket. This act seemed to relieve his feelings, because he said right away in a voice that sounded lighter and more contented:

"Well, I guess it is all for the best. I'll take it, and you can rest assured that you'll lose nothing by your kindness."

Their voices became lower again at this point, and Herbert, sorry for having remained so long, hurried back to bed and was soon in the land of slumber. Father, mother and son met at the breakfast table the next morning, and all seemed to be in a more cheerful frame of mind than they had been for some days. Mr. Harkins was bubbling over with good spirits. He turned to his wife in a laughing manner, and said:

"I've got a surprise for you this morning—a bit of good news that will make you feel good."

"What is it?" asked the wife curiously.

"Simply that I have the money and I am going to pay off that obligation to John Black before the clock strikes another hour."

The poor woman was so overjoyed at this unexpected news that she ran over and gave her husband a hearty kiss.

"This is good news, David," she said. "How on earth did you manage to raise the money in such a short time?"

"Oh ho!" he replied merrily; "it's news you are after, is it? Well you can't have it just now. This money came from a gentleman who is a very good friend of mine. His name will have to remain a secret for the present at least."

Herbert sat and listened to this conversation with a feeling of dismay. He felt like crying out and telling his father that he had been present at the mysterious midnight interview and had heard things that were not intended for his ears; but his lips refused to frame the words, and he sat there feeling very mean and very guilty. Finally both conscience and curiosity got the better of him. He made up his mind to confess his little indiscretion—for it was not anything more serious than an indiscretion—and then to ask his father to tell him the name of the strange man who had appeared at such an unusual hour and under such unusual circumstances. Mr. Harkins had his hat and coat on preparing to leave the house when Herbert arose from the table and said to him in a voice that quivered with nervousness:

"Father, I could not sleep last night."

"I am very sorry to hear that, my son," was the kindly reply. "Probably you are not feeling well. You had better stop in and see Dr. Smith on your way from school this afternoon."

"No, no; it's not that," stammered Herbert; "it's something I want to tell you. When I found that I could not sleep I got out of bed—"

"I am in a hurry now, Herbert," exclaimed his father, talking very rapidly and moving towards the door. "I must get down and see Mr. Coke. You can tell me this story when you come home from school this afternoon."

And the next moment the street door closed with a bang and Mr. Harkness was on his way to the bank. Herbert sat down in a chair feeling very much disappointed. He felt somehow or other that his father had become involved, and if he had been able to speak, that much mystery might have been dissipated.

CHAPTER V
IN WHICH DAVID HARKINS BECOMES THE VICTIM OF PECULIAR CIRCUMSTANCES

David Harkins left his home that morning, walking rapidly and gaily humming a tune to himself. He felt better and happier than he had for many weeks before. The thought of canceling the note and freeing himself from the obligation which he was under to John Black lifted an immense weight from his mind and enabled him to take a cheerful view of life. As he walked along he mentally matured plans for increasing his income during the year to come and placing his family in a position where they would not be compelled to feel concerned regarding the future.

In a few minutes he reached the office of Horace Coke, the lawyer, who was installed in a little second story room of a modest house on the main street. The apartment was very much like the lawyer—simple and old-fashioned, but entirely adequate for the needs of the law. There was a plain, flat-top desk, littered with legal papers. An office boy who hoped eventually to become a member of the bar, sat copying a deed; and the silence in the room was broken by the steady scratching of his pen. The shelves about the room were filled with law books covered with calfskin and bearing their titles in little gold letters on a slip of black over what might be called their backbones. Mr. Coke himself was puffing away at a big black cigar—which, by the way, was his only dissipation. He was looking over some papers when David Harkins entered the room, but jumped from his chair immediately and greeted the newcomer with a hearty:

"Hello there, Dave! What's bringing you out so early in the morning?"

"Some legal business, Horace," replied the other laughingly.

"I am sorry to hear that," said the venerable attorney, shaking his head in a doubtful manner. "I always advise my friends to keep out of the law. It's a bad business. It takes up all your money, and rarely gives you any good results."

"That sounds like queer talk for a man who depends on the law for his livelihood."

Horace Coke laughed heartily at this retort, and said:

"It does sound queer, doesn't it? But I don't talk that way to everybody. Of course, if people will get into trouble and will invoke the law, I might as well take their money and attend to their business as the next one; but I satisfy my conscience by advising all of my friends to keep out of the law, because as I said before, it's a mighty bad business."

Then the good-natured counsellor dropped into his chair and indulged in another hearty laugh. It was one of the oddities of his nature that he should be continually berating the profession of which he was such an ornament and for which he really had a deep reverence.

"But not to get off the subject," added Mr. Harkins, "I would like to inform you that I have come here to pay off that note to John Black. Under ordinary circumstances I would go to the bank to transact this business; but as long as Mr. Black has found it necessary to employ a lawyer to secure his money, I felt that it was proper to come here and pay you."

The lawyer looked at David Harkins searchingly through his eye-glasses. He was silent for a moment, and then said in a low voice, in marked contrast with his jolly manner of a few minutes before:

"See here, Dave, can you spare this money? I don't believe you can, and I hate to see a man pressed. If you say the word, I'll go over to old Black and try to get an extension on the note."

"Not at all," was the cheerful rejoinder. "I do not desire an extension; I want to pay it and get it off my mind forever."

Mr. Coke walked over to Harkins and taking him by the hand, exclaimed in his cheery voice:

"Congratulations, old man! I am glad to hear you talk in that way, and I am mighty glad to know that you were able to raise the money in such a short time. It will not only be a good thing to pay off the note, but it will be the means of establishing your credit in Cleverly. There's nothing like a reputation for a man, and if you can get a good one it is liable to stick to you just as well as a bad one."

The two men sat down at the desk together, and after the necessary papers had been prepared and signed, Mr. Harkins handed over one thousand dollars in fresh banknotes.

Half an hour later the lawyer put his hat and coat on and started towards the bank where he had an appointment with John Black. The door was closed when he arrived; but following his usual custom he entered without knocking. The banker's back was turned to him at the time, and when he heard the door open and close, Mr. Black cried out in a harsh voice:

"Who's that? What are you doing there?"

"It is only I, John," said the lawyer. "I came here to attend to a little matter of business."

"Oh!" exclaimed the banker, changing his tone slightly at the sight of the lawyer. "I thought it was one of those impudent clerks coming in here without being civil enough to knock at the door."

After this he started to walk up and down the office, stamping his feet and frowning in a very ugly manner. His expression was forbidding, and Mr. Coke looked at him in astonishment.

"What's the matter, Black?" asked the lawyer. "You don't seem to be in a very good humor this morning."

"Good humor? I should say not. I've got a good notion to leave this town. A man's property isn't safe over night. You get no protection. You pay big taxes and put up with all sorts of inconveniences, and what do you get in return? That's what I would like to know; what do you get in return?"

"Why what in the world are you driving at?" asked the lawyer; "what has happened?"

"Happened? Why everything's happened. Some thief entered my house last night, got into the library, broke open my desk and stole a package of money that I had put there for safe keeping over night. What do you think of that? Wouldn't you say that something had happened if your house had been broken into and your desk had been rifled? Wouldn't you, I say? Wouldn't you?"

"Why, yes," said the lawyer, staring at his client. "I suppose I should say that something had happened under those circumstances. But have you any clue to the robbery?"

"Clue! Clue!" retorted the banker, with his habit of repeating words. "Certainly not. How could you expect me to have a clue in a town like this? The police officials are no good, never were any good, and never will be any good."

"But have you any hope of recovering your money?"

"Hope? Certainly I have hope. I am going to recover that money if it costs every other cent that I have in the world. I don't propose to sit down like a lamb and be fleeced. Do you think that I am that kind of a man? Do you?"

"No," said the lawyer, "I do not. I am very sorry to hear about your loss; but I don't suppose there is any use crying over spilt milk."

"Spilt milk! What do you mean by that? How can you talk about a large amount of money as if it were spilt milk? What do you mean anyhow?"

"Oh," said the lawyer, "that was simply a little illustration of mine. You see the moral is a good one."

"Hump! I don't think it's good at all, and I don't like to hear you talk in that way." Then after a momentary pause, "But what is it you want? Why did you come here?"

"I came with some good news," said the lawyer. "David Harkins called on me this morning and paid off that note of a thousand dollars, and I have brought the money to you."

The crafty face of the banker lighted up with surprise at this announcement. It was so unexpected that he hardly knew what to say in reply. Finally he managed to remark:

"Paid you? Paid you this morning, did he? I wonder where he got the money."

"I am sure I do not know," said the lawyer, "and really I don't think it makes much difference as long as you get the amount of your note."

The two men sat down at the desk together, and the lawyer, after some preliminary remarks, handed over the money to the banker. The minute it was laid before him he jumped with a start.

"Why, this is all new money," he exclaimed. "That's just the kind of money that was taken from me last night. I don't believe Dave Harkins came by that money honestly. It makes him look like a thief. It was probably done by that smart boy of his."

"I wouldn't say that," cried the lawyer, trying to pacify the banker.

"But I will say it. Both father and son have a grudge against me, and I don't believe they would hesitate at anything to get even."

"But my dear sir," remarked the lawyer in a soothing tone, "you have made a very rash assertion, and you have absolutely nothing to base it upon."

John Black was silent for a moment, and then suddenly turning around, he said in a harsh tone:

"Did you get that money direct from David Harkins?"

"I did," was the response.

"Then," exclaimed the banker in a tone of triumph, "that proves my suspicion. The money that was taken out of my desk consisted of ten $100 bills, and the money you have just given me is made up exactly of ten $100 bills. That satisfies me."

"It is a coincidence," admitted the lawyer.

"Coincidence," snorted the banker, "it's sufficient to convict the man. It satisfies me, and it ought to be enough to satisfy any other man with brains."

"I wouldn't be too hasty," suggested the lawyer. "There is nothing to be gained by acting in that manner."

"Hasty? Don't talk about being hasty. I am going to have justice no matter who is injured; and I don't want to be soft-soaped out of doing the right thing. I am going to act, and I am going to act quickly."

"But, my dear sir," said the lawyer, persisting in his objections, "you must have proof; don't you understand that? You must have proof before you can accuse a man."

John Black was in a terrible rage by this time. He paced up and down the office rapidly, and then standing in front of the lawyer and raising his finger in a threatening way, exclaimed:

"I'll have proof all right. The proof will be a warrant for the arrest of David Harkins on the charge of stealing my money."

"I am sorry to hear you talk that way," said the lawyer, "I think you are making a mistake. But, however, you are master of your own actions. When do you propose to do this?"

"Within twenty-four hours," replied the other solemnly. "If you want to, you can serve a warning on Dave Harkins, and if he will restore my money at once I may be merciful to him; but if not, he must take the consequences. In any event he will have to make up his mind within the next twenty-four hours."

CHAPTER VI
IN WHICH DAVID HARKINS QUITS THIS LIFE AND TAKES HIS SECRET WITH HIM

News travels quickly in a small town. Before breakfast the following morning it was very generally reported that John Black had been robbed, and that he was going to issue a warrant for the arrest of David Harkins. The report shocked most of those who heard it. John Black was a hard man, and more than one of the citizens of Cleverly had felt the force of his iron hand.

He worked incessantly, and never spent a penny unless it was absolutely necessary. Such a man may be considered just; but he is bound to be unpopular. David Harkins, on the contrary, was well liked by all who knew him. He was on the best of terms with his neighbors, and always had time for a kind word to everyone he met—man, woman and child.

The people therefore were disposed to suspend judgment until they had heard both sides of the story. While David Harkins was at the table Horace Coke drove up, and asked to have a minute's conversation. As soon as they were alone he said hastily:

"Have you heard the rumors?"

"I have," responded Harkins, "and I consider them scandalous. I wonder where such malicious stories could originate?"

"That's easily told," replied the lawyer. "They come from no less a person than John Black."

"How dare he say such things!" exclaimed Harkins with passion.

For answer the lawyer told him the details of his interview with the banker and the singular likeness between the banknotes that had been stolen and the money which had been used to pay off the note.

David Harkins listened in astonishment, and when Coke had concluded, said:

"But even that doesn't justify Black in slandering me."

"Certainly not; but you must agree that the coincidence is not only remarkable, but could be construed as suspicious."

"But my part of the transaction was perfectly straight."

"I'm sure of that," responded Coke with fervor, "and that's why I'm here this morning. Let me state the case in a nutshell. You have been foolish enough to make an enemy of a powerful and wealthy man. You have borrowed money of him. He demands the payment of the money from you in the belief that you are penniless and cannot comply with his demand. His house is entered and robbed of a thousand dollars. The next morning you pay him a thousand dollars in bills identical to those stolen from him."

"But there are thousands of such bills in circulation."

"True; but the thing for you to do is to shut the mouth of gossip at once. That can be done in a very simple manner. All you have to do is to prove what is known in the law as an alibi. Tell where you got the money and produce the man who gave it to you."

Harkins shook his head sadly at this.

"Your suggestion seems simple enough; but I fear I cannot comply with it."

"Why not?" in manifest astonishment.

"Because it was given to me in confidence and with the understanding that the name of the donor should not be divulged."

"But it came from a friend?"

"One of the best I have in the world."

"Well, he would surely not permit you to rest under a shadow for the sake of a foolish promise. Go to him at once and get a release from your pledge to silence."

"I'm afraid it's too late," said Harkins gravely. "He was to start for England this very day. However, your advice is good. I'll hire a team and try to reach him. If I succeed I will report to you this afternoon."

As soon as Mr. Coke departed, Herbert made an effort to tell his father the story of his indiscretion in listening at the doorway on the occasion of the midnight visit of the mysterious stranger. But once again Mr. Harkins was too busy to stop and listen, and father and son parted without that exchange of confidence which would have done so much to clear up an embarrassing situation. Mr. Harkins went to the nearest livery stable and soon had a one-horse buggy harnessed and ready for the road. He told no one his destination, but whipping up the horse, passed down the main streets, out into the outskirts of the town and was soon lost to view.

It was late in the afternoon when he returned, and then the wheels of the carriage were covered with mud and the horse was covered with lather as if he had traveled far and fast that day. There was a careworn look about David Harkins' eyes and a drooping of the lips that betokened disappointment. He drove back over the same streets whence he had taken his departure in the morning, nodding pleasantly to several acquaintances he passed on the way.

Just when he was in sight of the livery stable, a sudden gust of wind raised a cloud of dust that blinded animals and pedestrians alike. This was followed by another, and the second squall carried in its wake a batch of old newspapers and sent them eddying about in the air like some strange craft in a whirlpool. One of the papers struck the horse square in the eye. The animal, already frightened by the wind and dust, raised up on its haunches and gave a shrill neigh. Harkins grasping the reins tightly, pulled it down to earth again. But the moment the horse's feet struck the ground it darted off like a flash and went tearing down the street at an insane gait. The driver kept cool and self contained. Standing on the floor of the carriage and leaning over the dashboard he pulled at the lines with all his strength.

Just when he felt that the animal was being brought into subjection, the lines gave a snap and broke, leaving him thrown back on the seat with two useless bits of leather in his hand. He was as helpless as a seaman without a rudder, or more so. The horse released from the grasp of the driver, redoubled its speed and kept on its way like mad. Harkins, now alarmed, considered the advisability of jumping out of the vehicle in order to avert a worse fate. But while he was debating the situation the horse solved it for him. Coming to a cross street it swerved in its furious career and turned the corner. The suddenness of the move swung the buggy from one side of the street to the other, and on its rebound it struck an iron lamp-post, smashing the frail vehicle to pieces and throwing David Harkins head first on to the sidewalk.

A crowd collected immediately and several men hurried to the assistance of the stricken man. He was insensible, and his breath came in short, sharp gasps. A stretcher was procured, and he was carried to his home. A physician was telephoned for, and he arrived at the home simultaneously with the men who were carrying the prostrate form. The doctor worked unceasingly for nearly an hour, and at the end of that time announced that his patient must have absolute quiet and that no one must attempt to speak to him for the present.

Horace Coke, who had arrived at the house, was very much distressed over the accident and showed especial pain over the doctor's order.

"Doctor," he said, "couldn't I ask him one question?"

"My dear sir," answered the physician pityingly, "you can do as you please; but the instant you or anyone else disobeys my orders I will give this case up and will not answer for the consequences."

"Is it that bad?" asked the lawyer.

"It couldn't be worse," replied the doctor; "he only regained consciousness a few minutes ago. I succeeded in putting him into a light slumber. If he rests undisturbed for an hour I may save his life."

Herbert slipped quietly out of the room while the two men were speaking.

"He is still sleeping," he said to the doctor.

The doctor shot a sharp glance at the boy.

"I hope you didn't attempt to speak to him," rather sternly.

"Certainly not," replied Herbert, flushing up at this reflection upon his good sense. Slowly, slowly, the minutes ticked by.

A few of the neighbors remained in the parlor. The doctor and Mrs. Harkins alone remained in the sick room. A half hour elapsed. It began to look as if the life might be saved.

Presently the door opened and a young girl attired in a dark suit entered the room. Although youthful, she had the air of restfulness usually found only in persons of more mature years. She had great black eyes now full of sympathy with those in the room. Her dark, glossy hair parted in the middle, emphasized the extreme whiteness of her broad forehead. This was Mary Black, daughter of the banker, and sister of Arthur Black. She glanced about the apartment until her glance rested upon Herbert, and going up to him, put her hand in his with such frankness and tenderness as to bring tears to his eyes. He stepped to one side of the room. She was the first to speak.

"Herbert, I feel for you very, very much," she said in a low, melodious voice. "Mother would not rest until I had come over here to inquire how your father was getting on. Indeed we all feel for you and your mother very much. Father was anxious also."

She was quick to see that Herbert's face clouded up at the mention of her father, and hastened to add:

"That is what I wished to speak about particularly. I know that your father and my father had words; but I can assure you that there is no ill feeling on father's part now. I talked with him long and earnestly, and he finally consented to permit me to come over here and say this to your father. The moment he is able to see anyone, I want to tell him this."

"You are an angel," murmured Herbert. "I don't thank your father for this visit, but I am very, very grateful to you."

Just then Mrs. Harkins stepped out of the room, and Mary made haste to repeat to her what she had already told Herbert. The face of the older woman softened at the kind words that were poured into her ears, and in a moment the girl and the mother were in each other's arms, indulging in one of those crys which do so much to relieve the tension of grief and sorrow.

But Mary Black did not waste much time in useless tears. She quickly dried her eyes, and turning to Mrs. Harkins, said with energy:

"Now, I'm going to make myself useful; tell me what to do first."

Mrs. Harkins smiled through her tears at this manifestation of industry. But she felt relieved to know that feminine hands and feminine eyes would be in charge of her house while she remained at the bedside of her stricken husband. Mary Black, during that hour of anxiety and for many days afterward, proved herself a genuine angel of mercy. Those who gazed at her knew that while her nature was kind and gentle she was yet resolute and determined.

The minutes went by and those who were assembled in the outer room kept anxious watch on the door leading to the sick chamber. All instinctively realized that a crisis was at hand, and that it was to be decided very shortly. Presently there was a movement within and the doctor came out, supporting Mrs. Harkins on his shoulder. A hush went over the little circle.

"What is it, doctor?" asked Mr. Coke, voicing the question that hung unspoken on the lips of all the others.

The doctor looked at his questioner in silence for a moment, and then said impressively:

"He is dead!"

A convulsive sob from the newly made widow brought Mary Black and some of the neighbors to her side in an instant. While they were leading the weeping woman up to her room, the doctor noted the questioning look in Mr. Coke's eyes.

"It came very suddenly," he said; "all was over in an instant. He died without opening his lips."

Herbert, who was standing in the rear of the room unobserved, heard this with blanched face and parched throat. He realized that the death of his father marked an epoch in his life. He felt that he had lost his dearest friend. Yet the tears would not come to his strained, glassy eyes. He was amazed that his heart beat on as before. All that he was conscious of was a strange, unnatural feeling of numbness.

CHAPTER VII
IN WHICH HERBERT MEETS ADVERSITY AND LEARNS THE MEANING OF HARD WORK

The Harkins home was a very desolate place for many days after the funeral. Mary Black remained with the family for several days, moving about noiselessly and attending to the multitude of details which would otherwise go neglected at such a sad period. After the first sharp grief had worn away, Herbert and his mother sat down and talked over their prospects for the future. Mr. Harkins had been prudent enough to leave a small insurance policy, made out to the order of Mrs. Harkins, and this money proved to be of immediate assistance to the widow.

Mrs. Harkins was a firm believer in the value of education, and felt that it was her duty to give Herbert all the schooling that was possible even if it was necessary to make a personal sacrifice to do so. She insisted upon his going to school for at least a year after the death of his father. He did so and made gratifying progress; but he was now old enough to appreciate the responsibility that rested upon him as an only son, so just before the close of the school term he went to his mother and said:

"See here, mother, I've got to help you. There is no possible way out of it. If I can do so and continue going to school, all right; if not, I will never return to the school."

"What you say is probably true, my boy," replied his mother; "but the question is what to do and how to do it."

"Well, suppose we settle it now," said Herbert resolutely.

"Can't we postpone the thing for a day or so?" asked Mrs. Harkins anxiously.

"Yes," responded Herbert, "we could; but there is nothing like doing to-day, instead of postponing until to-morrow."

"In that case," said his mother, "I think you had better continue going to school until the close of the present term, at least."

"That's bully!" exclaimed Herbert heartily. "I am going to put my mind on my studies, and I don't think I'll be a blockhead when the term is over."

"That's true," responded his mother sadly. "But there is another feature of the case that gives me great sorrow."

"What is it?" asked Herbert.

"Your college education," replied his mother. "You know it was your father's fondest wish, as well as my own, that after leaving the Cleverly School you should take the four year course at St. Joseph's College. I don't see how it can be done now."

Herbert hung his head and said nothing. The necessity of abandoning this cherished project was a severer blow to him than he was willing to admit to his mother. He had dreamed of a professional career and often thought that if he were able to go through the College he would be fitted to take the necessary examination for either the legal or the medical profession. But now his dream was over; he was an only son, and his duty to his mother was clear. Mr. and Mrs. Harkins were the parents of three other children; but each of these had died in early infancy; and now the great heap of earth which covered the remains of the lamented father of the house was in close proximity to the three little mounds which were watered and kept green by the tender care and love which only a mother can understand and give. Herbert thought of all these things as he sat silent that day. Presently he lifted his head and spoke to his mother.

"Mother, I am old enough to understand my duty. I wanted to go to the College very, very much; but now I know that it is impossible. We must meet adversity, and meet it bravely."

Her only answer was to embrace the boy who was acquiring manliness at such a rapid rate.

The school question for the term having been settled, the next question was to consider what steps could be taken to increase their very small income. The subject having been opened, was discussed at various times during the next two weeks. There was a twenty acre farm adjoining the little home of the Harkins. It came up against the little vegetable garden which Mr. Harkins had cultivated with care and profit during his lifetime. The tenant of the large tract had been unfortunate, and he was anxious to sub-let his lease for a very modest sum of money. Herbert consulted with Mr. Coke, the lawyer, regarding the matter, and after some days it was decided to purchase the lease, which had about two years to run.

The first step in the new life was the engaging of a farmhand to do the heavy work on the twenty acre tract. A reliable, industrious man was secured for a very reasonable amount of wages; but with the understanding that he would be kept for at least two years. The work was begun under pleasant auspices. After it had proceeded a few weeks, it was decided that Herbert should get as much schooling as he could in the meantime. It must be admitted that he attended school rather irregularly during this period. It was at this time of his life that he learned in a manner never to be forgotten that this is a world of hard work. Often he got out of bed before dawn in order to ride the horse to plough among the growing corn, potatoes and hops. The program was to get as much ploughed by ten o'clock in the morning as could be hoed during the remainder of that day. After this Herbert would start for school, where he sometimes arrived as the afternoon session was half through. In winter his work was lighter, but the snow was often deep and drifted. The cold was intense, the north wind piercing and his clothing so thin that he felt real discomfort.

At night, when his work was over and he had a spare hour, he made it a habit to study the art of debating. The first book he ever owned was the "Columbian Orator," which was given to him by his uncle one winter as he lay very sick with the measles. In the natural order of things Herbert soon became recognized as the head of the house, and his mother leaned on him for advice and accepted his decisions without question. At the end of the first year, when Herbert balanced his carefully kept accounts, he found that they had come out just even. It was a little bit discouraging to find that they had made no profit from their hard work; but it was a real consolation to know that there had been no further drain upon the small amount of money which Mrs. Harkins had laid aside from her husband's insurance policy.

At the beginning of the second year of farming, Herbert learned to his amazement that the man from whom they had purchased the unexpired lease owed money to a number of tradesmen for implements and supplies. These men came to him and demanded the payment of their claims; but he was neither able nor willing to satisfy them. Herbert and his man had finished their summer tilling and their haying when a heavy rain set in near the end of August. The dreary character of the weather seemed to fill him with a foreboding of approaching calamity. One night Mr. Coke came to him with tidings that their ill fortune was about to culminate. The following morning the sheriff and some other officials, with two or three of the principal creditors, appeared and after formally demanding payment of their claims, proceeded to levy on the farm stock, implements, household effects and other worldly possessions, coupled with a threat of arrest and imprisonment for the original tenant who was invisible for some days.

Herbert and his mother stopped with a friendly neighbor while the work of levying went on. In the meantime Mr. Coke had not been idle. He denounced the proceedings as an outrage, saying that it was wrong both in law and morals to hold Herbert and his mother responsible for the faults or crimes of another. He did more than protest, however. He acted and acted promptly. He went into court, explained the matter very clearly to the Judge, and succeeded in obtaining an order by which the levy was stopped. Herbert and his mother immediately resumed their old life; but at the end of the year both decided that it would be advisable to quit farming, which in their circumstances offered little return for the hard labor involved.

The hired man, who had proven himself to be an unusually efficient and industrious man, still had two months of his time to run. He generously offered to release Herbert from this obligation; but the boy had inherited his father's trait of pluck and manliness, declined to accept the offer. He had heard that one of the merchants in the town who had purchased a large amount of ground on the other side of the railroad, was anxious to have someone undertake the job of clearing up fifty acres of the wildest land. Herbert informed his assistant of that fact, and said that if he was willing to undertake the work he would guarantee to give him all that they had contracted to pay in the beginning. It was in November, and when the man and boy started to work the snow was just going and the water and slush in some places were knee deep.

Both were resolute, but they were indifferent choppers compared with those who usually grapple with forests, and the job looked so formidable that farmers and others passing along the turnpike were accustomed to halt and predict that Herbert would be a grown man before he saw the end of the job. But his fighting blood was up and he determined to plod along without rest until the work was accomplished. So they continued cutting trees and bushes, chopping up grown trunks into small lengths, digging out rotten pines from the soil where they had imbedded themselves, burning the brush and worthless sticks, and carting home such wood as served for fuel. So they persevered until the job was finally completed. Herbert received $200 for the work; and after paying the hired man the $60 that was his due he had $140 left to put in the family fund. There was still a balance to their credit. Herbert was very glad the work was finished. At times he felt that he would give way under the strain, but pluckily refused to do so. Frequently at night the sharp lances of the Canadian thistles had to be dug out of his festered feet with needles; but he had the stuff in him of which successful men are made. However, two years of this sort of toil were sufficient, and at the end of that time he cheerfully marked "the end" at the conclusion of his experience at farming.

CHAPTER VIII
HERBERT BECOMES AMBITIOUS AND IS FASCINATED BY THE SMELL OF PRINTERS' INK

From the time that he was first able to spell and connect one word with another, Herbert was fascinated by the sight of a printed page. If he saw a circular or a fragment of newspaper on the sidewalk he was impelled to pick it up and read its contents. The weekly paper was a rare treat to him and he perused its columns from the first page to the last, until he knew the contents almost by heart. The sight of a book of fiction or adventure or biography was one of the greatest joys on earth to him, and he eagerly devoured everything of that kind that came in his way. Early in his school-days he had written little essays which after being read in secret, many times, were finally consigned to the flames as being unworthy of publicity.

The town, among its other places and things of interest, possessed a weekly newspaper known as the Cleverly Banner. Herbert never passed the office of this newspaper without being filled with a wild desire to be on the inside instead of the outside of the building. Frequently he stood looking in the window watching the old-fashioned press as it slowly ground out the regular weekly edition. Once or twice he had occasion to call at the office of the Banner with reference to some printing that was being done there, and on such occasions he was thrown into transports of delight. The smell of the ink, the sound of the presses, and the sight of the freshly printed pages sent him into an ecstacy that was almost heavenly in its pleasure.

When he decided to quit farming his eye and heart unconsciously turned towards the little newspaper office. One morning he heard that an apprentice was needed there, he hastened to make application for the position. The building occupied by the Banner set back on a little lot facing the main street of the town. It was a two story and a half dwelling, and an old faded wooden sign over the doorway announced the name of the paper and informed the residents that "Job printing of all kinds could be furnished on short notice." The building itself was half rotted away from age and want of paint. One editor and one owner after another had succeeded to the Banner; but it had never occurred to any of them that it would be a good stroke of business policy to repair or at least paint the exterior of the building.

The first floor of the Banner office was taken up with a little counter where such business as was transacted with the public might be cared for. The remainder of the room was occupied by a very large old-fashioned printing press. It worked very slowly, and as a consequence had to go steadily two or three days a week in order to turn out the edition of the paper. The second floor, which resembled a hay loft more than a place of business, was utilized as the editorial and composing room. An old-fashioned stove in the centre of the room threw out a heat that made the apartment decidedly uncomfortable at times. A big, sleek cat dozing placidly beneath this stove was one of the permanent fixtures of the room.

It was quite early in the morning when Herbert called at the Banner office, and he did not find anyone on the first floor. He rapped on the counter to attract attention, and presently a voice from upstairs called out in clear, loud tones:

"Come upstairs."

He climbed up the rude stairway slowly, and finally emerged into the editorial and composing room. An elderly man sat in an old-fashioned armchair in front of a little desk with its top sloping very much like the desks used in some schools. He was writing rapidly and pausing every now and then to dip his pen into a big ink-pot which stood by his side. Visitors to the Banner office were well acquainted with that enormous ink-stand. It had been used by the various editors from the time of the foundation of the Banner and went back so far that its origin must finally have been lost in the mists of antiquity. When the industrious writer had finished a sentence or a paragraph to his satisfaction he wheeled about in his chair and expectorated a mouthful of tobacco juice into an ample cuspidor which stood on the other side of the desk. He had a shock of snow white hair, very much in disorder, caused no doubt from his habit of running his fingers through his hair when in search of a fugitive thought. He was in his shirt sleeves, which was his usual habit, for he always protested that it was not possible for a man to do his best work harnessed up in a coat and vest. Such was Noah Brooks, the editor of the Cleverly Banner, and one of the characters of the town. He looked up from his work as Herbert entered, and said:

"Hello there, young man! What can I do for you?"

"I want you to give me a job," said Herbert simply.

This reply seemed to amaze the editor, for he laid down his pen, pushed back his chair, and placing his feet on the desk before him, looked at Herbert with a good-natured smile. It seemed almost a minute before he spoke. When he did it was to say:

"So you want a job, do you? Well, that's a laudable ambition; but I am afraid you have come to the wrong place."

"I am sorry to hear that," said Herbert.

Noah Brooks looked at Herbert again before replying, and then moving slightly and raising the index finger of his right hand, he pointed to the rear of the room and said:

"Do you see those fellows over there?"

Herbert looked around and saw a man engaged in setting type, while a boy with a great big ink roller in one hand was engaged in taking a proof of a circular that was about to be printed.

"Yes sir," he answered obediently; "I see them."

"Well, do you know," said the old gentleman with a chuckle, "that about all those two fellows do is to sit around and wait for Saturday night in order to draw their salaries."

The humor of this seemed to appeal to the speaker so strongly that he had to pause and engage in a hearty laugh before proceeding. The man and the boy did not appear to be offended. On the contrary, they laughed too, as if they were accustomed to the good-natured jests of their employer.

"I am very sorry," said Herbert, breaking the silence; "but I was really anxious to get employment on this paper—I have long wished to enter the newspaper business."

"Is that so? Do you know anything about the business?"

"No," said Herbert; "I am entirely ignorant of it; but I felt that I could learn."

"That's the way to talk," was the hearty reply. "The only way to learn to do a thing is to do it. I think you would pan out all right in an office of this kind; but I am sorry to say we have no opening at the present time."

Herbert said "Good-by" quietly; but once out of the building he felt very much depressed at his failure to secure a situation. He did not tell his mother of his adventure, not wishing to annoy her with anything that was not of a cheerful nature. During the next few months he managed to earn a small amount of money by odd bits of employment that were furnished to him through Horace Coke, the lawyer; but as he had no taste for the law he did not feel very much encouraged over this occasional work. His mind still dwelt upon the newspaper business.

One evening he wrote a little item describing an entertainment given at the Cleverly High School, and mailed it to the office of the Banner, without indicating the name or address of the writer. After he had sent this little message on its way, he was figuratively speaking, on pins and needles until the next issue of the Cleverly Banner should appear. On the date of its regular issue, he hurried home in order to get the paper as soon as possible. He was disappointed. It had not arrived. Unable to wait, he rushed to the post office, and securing the paper, he eagerly tore off the wrapping and opened the page which contained the local news. What he found there caused his face to flush scarlet. The little item that he had written with such care was reproduced, word for word, as he had penned it, without a change of any kind. He felt so glad that he could have shouted for joy. Several other persons were in the post office, and he looked around at them as if to see whether they had read his secret; but apparently no one was paying any attention to him. He walked home in a fever of happiness, and it was only by the strongest effort on his part that he refrained from telling his mother about the incident.

Naturally he continued to send little items to the paper from week to week. Sometimes they failed to appear. On such occasions he felt a sense of loss and disappointment that was far out of proportion to the importance of the subject. But when the paragraphs did appear that feeling of elation and joy returned to him on each occasion.

Finally he determined to call at the office of the Banner once more. It was just possible that there might be an opening, and he made up his mind not to miss it merely for the sake of asking. The venerable editor with the snow white hair was in his place as usual. He recognized Herbert immediately, and cried out:

"Hello young man! I see you are here again."

"Yes sir," replied Herbert. "I do not want to be a bore, but I felt that it would be all right to inquire whether an opportunity had arisen by which I could secure employment on the Banner."

Once again the old man looked at him in that quizzical manner.

"Perseverance wins, boy," he said, "and you have won. I do need somebody. My apprentice has left me very suddenly, and I think I can make use of you. He only got four dollars a week. I know that will be pretty small for you; but I can afford to give you six dollars, and if you are willing to take it the job is yours."

Herbert could not conceal the pleasure that he felt.

"I will be delighted to accept," he said. "When do you want me to begin, and what may my duties be?"

"You can begin to-morrow morning at eight o'clock," was the response; "and your duties at first will consist of sweeping out the office, serving the Banner every week, working the printing press, and making yourself generally useful. That does not sound very poetic, does it? But you will find that it will prove a very useful discipline and may be valuable to you later in life."

Herbert began his work the following morning and did everything in his power to give satisfaction to his employer. If he swept out the office, he did it so carefully as to win the praise of the journeyman printer. When he served the papers, he did it with such accuracy as to merit the approval of the editor. This continued for several weeks, and at the end of that time he began to contribute little local items to the paper, much to the satisfaction of Mr. Brooks. In the meantime Mr. Anderson had opened a night school in the town, and Herbert resolved to attend the sessions of this school in order to perfect his education as much as possible.

Towards the close of the winter Mr. Brooks complimented Herbert by authorizing him to write the Irvington letter for the Banner. Irvington was the adjoining town, and by this new arrangement Herbert had to go there for the items regularly every week. He walked there and back in mid-winter in order to obtain this copy, and although the weather was sometimes very severe, he never complained. Under his arrangement with Mr. Brooks, he was to remain at the office of the Cleverly Banner until he was twenty years of age. Incidentally he was initiated into the mystery of typesetting, for the Banner, although progressive in some ways, had not yet reached the dignity of typesetting machines. The printing press gave him more trouble than any other part of his work. On the days that he had to assist in working the press his hands were blistered and his back lamed by constant stooping. Yet he was always kindly treated by those in authority, and in return merited their confidence and good will.

Late one afternoon on his way home he met Mary Black, who was as sweet and kind and tender as ever. Her first thought was about his new position.

"Herbert, I hear that you are connected with the Banner."

"Yes," he said modestly, "that is true."

"Are you the editor?"

"Not exactly."

"But what do you write for the paper?"

"When I do write," he said with a little hesitancy, "it is usually the local paragraphs."

"Did you write the account of the last entertainment at the Cleverly High School?"

"Yes," he replied, with an inquiring look in his eyes.

"Oh!" she exclaimed impulsively, "I think that that was just splendid. It was one of the nicest things I ever read."

Herbert flushed with conscious pride at this unexpected praise. He tried to turn it off by saying that it was only an ordinary piece of work; but as he walked away he had a difficult time in smothering the feeling of pride that rose in his breast in spite of himself. He could scarcely eat his supper that night so strong was the feeling of elation within him, and even as late as bedtime the recollection of the praise given him so sweetly filled him with as much delight as if he had suddenly fallen heir to a great fortune.

CHAPTER IX
HAVING BECOME A NEWSPAPER WRITER, HERBERT LOOKS FOR NEW WORLDS TO CONQUER

In the early part of the winter Mr. Brooks was taken ill with what the doctor diagnosed as grippe. He thought at first that he would be about in a few days; but the days lengthened into weeks, and even then the physician would not permit him to leave the house. In the beginning of his illness the editor did a great deal of his work at home, sending the copy to the office in time for the regular edition of the Banner. But as time wore on the medical man frowned upon this, declaring that it was retarding his recovery.

One day the editor sent for Herbert, and after some questions regarding himself and the office, said:

"Herbert, I'm going to place a new responsibility on you. The doctor has forbidden my doing any more writing. I want you to take my place. I want you to write the editorials and as many of the local items as possible. In short, I want you to manage the Banner until I am able to be about again. Will you do it?"

"Gladly," replied Herbert.

From that day he felt an added importance, although he did not show it by act or word. He must have had a natural instinct for the newspaper business, for everything moved along with remarkable smoothness and despite the fact that he had to labor incessantly he was fond of his work.

Subscribers noticed an improvement in the Banner. The local paragraphs became more numerous and were filled with human interest. The editorials also were crisp and to the point. Indeed they became a decided feature of the paper whereas they were formerly accepted as a painful necessity. One day an old reader of the paper who came in to renew his subscription to the paper, said:

"I want to congratulate you on the good paper you are getting out. This is especially true of the editorial columns. I find the comment on the news to be short and snappy. This is much better than the long articles which used to be more or less instructive, but generally as dull as sermons. How do you do it? You must have some secret method. What is it?"

Herbert smiled at this sweeping praise. He pointed to a little motto which hung over his desk.

"I don't know," he said, "unless it is because I follow the advice on that card."

The little inscription to which he pointed said simply:

"Brevity is the soul of wit."

"That is as true to-day," he remarked, "as when it was first penned by the great poet."

Herbert did not tell his caller one of the means he had used to arrive at such a desirable end. When he began writing editorials he found himself almost unconsciously padding them out to a half column and a column in length. He pondered long and earnestly over the means of breaking himself of the habit. Finally he hit on a plan which was as simple as it was effective. He cut his copy paper in such a length that it would not hold more than eight or ten lines. When he got an idea for an editorial comment, he endeavored to express it clearly and pointedly in the number of words that would go on the small sheet of paper. At first it was a very difficult task, but practice makes perfect, and at length he found that he could do it with comparative ease and eventually reached the state of things which had won him unstinted praise.

He had not been in charge of the Banner long before he realized that the local news was the most important thing in the paper to the people of Cleverly. Accordingly he bent all of his energies to the improvement of that department. He pressed the postmaster into his service. He induced some of the young men of the town to contribute, and as a result there was not a wedding, a birth or a funeral that was not fully reported in the Banner. He laid great stress on personal items, taking the ground that a pleasant reference to anyone not only interested the person mentioned, but also their relatives and friends as well as the people of the town. If a church raised its mortgage, or a citizen put an addition to his house, or the school gave an entertainment it was sure to be found in the local columns. It was not surprising, therefore, that the subscribers looked forward with eagerness for their paper and complained bitterly if, by chance, they failed to receive it.

Herbert avoided rumors and scandals with scrupulous care. He made up his mind that as long as he was at the helm such things would not find their way into the weekly. He remembered, with bitterness, the stories that had been circulated about his father, and while they had been well nigh forgotten by the people of the town, they were still treasured up in a corner of his memory. He frequently talked with his mother, and although she gave him no encouragement, persisted in a determination to clear his father's name.

"There was some strange mystery connected with father's last day," he said, "and I will never rest entirely happy until it has been fully cleared. I believe the suggestion that he stole that money was a base calumny, but I will not be content until the world is convinced that he was innocent."

His face would darken at this, and he would add:

"And when his innocence is proved the guilt of someone else will be established, and that person, whoever it may be, need expect no mercy from me."

One day when he had been talking in this strain his mother said:

"Herbert, I want you to drop this sort of thing. You are on the verge of man's estate and you should look forward and not backward. I feel the blot on your father's good name quite as keenly as you do, but I would be most unhappy if I thought you would permit it to embitter your life. This is a busy world, and the people in it—men and women—have little time for the person who is nursing a grievance."

"You mean well, mother," replied the young journalist, "but you do not realize the feeling I have. It is not a feeling of bitterness; it is not a grievance; it is a desire—a desire that will not be quenched—for justice. No matter where I go or what I may do, this desire remains with me, and some day it shall be gratified."

She stroked his hands fondly and looked at him with undisguised admiration.

"While you live your father will never die—you resemble him in more ways than one. Go ahead and carry out your own designs. I am content to have you do as you will."

In the meantime the circulation of the Banner was increasing by leaps and bounds. The job printing office was going at full speed. This condition of affairs began to show itself in the accounts. Noah Brooks, who was beginning to improve in health, noticed it with evident satisfaction.

"Herbert," he said when the young man visited him one day, "I am satisfied that you have made good. I have resolved to make your salary ten dollars a week. Probably you are worth more than that, but it is all I can do at present."

"It will be gratefully accepted," replied Herbert. "It is a proof that you are satisfied with my work, and that is compensation in itself."

During this time the young man, who was soon to celebrate his twenty-first birthday, had not neglected to advance himself in the art of writing. He felt that this was to be his trade, and that if a man devoted years to the work of becoming a proficient carpenter or bricklayer there was no reason why he should not also give time and study to the work of learning to write. He had left school, but Mr. Anderson, who had been his devoted friend from the time he had routed the other boys from the schoolhouse on "barring out day," very kindly offered to give him a special course of instruction in English composition. By this means the long winter passed away very quickly, and Herbert advanced rapidly in his chosen business.

One evening when Herbert came home from his studies, a little earlier than usual, he found Mary Black in the parlor with his mother. After the usual cordial greetings she said timidly:

"I hope you have forgiven us for the dreadful things that occurred before your father's death."

"We have nothing to forgive you for, Mary," said Herbert gently. "If there has been any obligation it is entirely on our side. I am sure that neither mother nor I can ever forget your kindness."

She flushed a little at this, and then after some hesitancy, said:

"It's not that. I know you have only kind feelings toward me. But I want you to be charitable to father and—and to Arthur."

She hung her head, and Herbert, a trifle embarrassed, made no reply. He glanced up and noticed that her eyes were red and her face careworn. His mother noticed the look, and quickly stepped in the breach.

"Mary is in trouble," she said; "Arthur left home last week and has not been heard of since then."

"Oh," cried Herbert impulsively, going up and taking her hands. "I am very, very sorry to hear this, and if I can assist you in any way you need only command me."

Her only reply was to weep quietly. Mrs. Harkins took her in her arms and soothed her with motherly kindness. Herbert felt quite awkward at this scene. First he stood on one foot and then on the other. Finally for want of something to say he exclaimed:

"You can rest assured that I have no feelings of resentment toward your father or Arthur. I was angry with them, very angry; but I am not vindictive."

He did not add that the fact that she was the daughter of one and the sister of the other caused him to utter such a generous sentiment.

"Have you any idea where Arthur has gone?" he asked a moment later.

"No," she replied; "that is what makes it so distressing. If it were not for the uncertainty we might feel resigned."

"Did anyone go with him?"

"We are not sure, but he was seen with Harry Adler just before he left."

"Oh!" exclaimed Herbert. "Then it's ten to one he has gone to New York. Adler has a perfect mania for that place."

"I'm sorry," ejaculated Mrs. Harkins, "because if that's so, Arthur is in very bad company in a very wicked place."

In spite of himself, Herbert had to laugh at the vehemence with which his mother uttered her sentiments. After some further conversation he said:

"I may be able to help you, Mary. You know Mr. Anderson has gone to New York to accept a position as teacher in a private academy. I'll write to him and ask him to keep on the lookout for Arthur. Of course New York is a big city and it seems like looking for a needle in a haystack, but it's just possible he may run across him. Anyhow it will do no harm to try."

The letter was dispatched that night. As he posted it Herbert little thought it was to be the messenger which was to summon him to newer, higher and more responsible duties. But a kind fate which conceals from us the misfortunes we are to undergo also hides from us the path which is to lead to happiness and prosperity. Although Noah Brooks had returned to the office and was able to resume his work, he insisted that Herbert should continue the writing he had been doing so well.

Three days later Herbert received a letter postmarked New York. He rightly surmised that it was from Mr. Anderson. It was brief and cordial. It said that he had heard nothing of Arthur Black, but that if he should run across him in the future he would immediately notify the family at Cleverly. There was a postscript to the letter, and unusual for a man's postscript, it contained the most important thing of all. Mr. Anderson said that he had become acquainted with the city editor of the Argus, one of the important daily newspapers of the metropolis, and that he had the disposal of a position on the local staff which would pay fifteen dollars a week at the start, with a prospect for promotion and increased salary at an early date. The teacher said that Herbert's letter had reached him opportunely and that he had strongly recommended his young friend for the position. The city editor, he added, would give him one week in which to either accept or decline the offer.

Herbert jumped at least two feet in the air when he had finished reading this letter. It offered him an opportunity he had secretly coveted for a long while. He hurried home to show the communication to his mother. Dinner had been served and she was waiting for him. As he took his place at the table, he tossed the envelope over to her.

"A letter from New York," he said.

She read it through carefully. When she reached the postscript a shadow crossed her face.

"What are you going to do about it?" she asked.

He appreciated fully the meaning of that question. He understood that the answer to it meant either the continuance of their present comfortable home life or a temporary painful separation. But he knew his mother well too, and he realized from her tone and manner that she did not intend to advise him one way or the other. She was interested in his welfare and would let him settle the question for himself. Nevertheless she waited, with some anxiety, for the reply. Herbert walked over and put his arms about her shoulders as if to reassure her, and then replied in a low tone:

"I will make my decision within twenty-four hours."

CHAPTER X
WHICH TELLS OF HOW HERBERT CAME TO LEAVE THE TOWN OF CLEVERLY

As soon as he arrived at the office of the Banner on the following morning, Herbert showed Noah Brooks the letter he had received from New York, and said he had not yet decided whether to accept or decline the proffer of the position on the New York Argus.

"It is not a matter of salary, Mr. Brooks," he said, "but the question of my future. The prospect of an opening in the metropolis is alluring, yet I dislike the idea of leaving Cleverly."

"Take your time and do the right thing, Herbert," said the veteran editor. "As you are aware, your time with me expired some months ago, and your further continuance depends entirely upon yourself. I am frank enough to say that there is not much chance of advancement here."

A few minutes later the young man left the office for the purpose of transacting some business with the postmaster of the town. That official had stepped out for the moment, but his clerk courteously invited Herbert to take a seat in his private office and await his return. For a few minutes the young man whiled away the time by idly turning over the pages of some newspapers that he found upon the postmaster's desk. Presently his attention was attracted by the sound of footsteps in the outside corridor. It was nearly mail time, and people were assembling for the purpose of receiving their letters and papers. The board partition between the private office and the outside room was very thin, and Herbert could hear bits of conversation. He paid no attention to them at first, but after a while the mention of his father's name caused him to prick up his ears in wonder. He recognized the voices of the two speakers; one was a well-to-do farmer named Bingham who operated an extensive place just outside of Cleverly; the other, John Peterson, a wholesale grocer, ranked among the leading citizens of the town. They were in a secluded corner of the post office, and after a while their conversation became quite animated. Bingham was doing most of the talking. He said very earnestly:

"I always liked Dave Harkins, and it has been a standing regret with me that the mystery of his last days was never cleared up."

"I have heard a great deal about that," responded Peterson, "but I have never been able to get head or tail of the affair. There was a mystery sure enough, and Harkins died under a cloud; but it was never explained to me by anyone who was in a position to talk about the matter."

"Well," replied the other slowly, "I can't say that I am an authority on the subject; yet I know some of the facts. It seems that old man Black took an unaccountable dislike to Dave Harkins and went to him and insisted upon the immediate repayment of a loan that he had made some time previous. Harkins was not supposed to have an extra dollar in the world. Yet he paid the loan in full the following day. That night—or rather the night before— Black's place was broken into and a bundle of money stolen. Now the curious part of the story is the allegation that the money which Harkins used to pay off his debt to Black, was the identical cash that was taken from Black's desk the night before. That is the shape the rumors took. For my part I don't believe it; and yet, unfortunately, Dave Harkins died before he could set himself straight with the community. His wife and son have never attempted to clear the matter up. Probably they are unable to do so. You don't suppose that Dave Harkins could have been tempted to take the money, do you?"

"Lord forbid," rejoined the other, "I believe that he was a thoroughly honest man; but the thing is to get other people to believe the same thing. A bit of scandal is a terrible thing; it may start out in the beginning no bigger than the tip end of a pin; but by the time it gets through growing it is taller than one of those skyscraping office buildings in New York. To tell you the truth I dislike to talk about such things. You are the first man I ever discussed the Harkins case with. Whenever the subject is brought up—and it has been mentioned to me once or twice—I always pooh-hooh it."

"What reminds you of it to-day?" inquired his companion.

"Young Harkins," was the prompt rejoinder. "I stopped in at the Banner office to congratulate old man Brooks on the way that young man was running the paper for him, and he astonished me by the news that young Harkins was likely to leave him. He's got an offer to go to New York and he's considering it just now. Do you think it is possible, Bingham, that this story concerning his father affects his standing in the community?"

"Undoubtedly," was the quick response. "A thing of that kind will never die a natural death in a little town like this. It has either got to be cleared up and ripped out of existence, root and branch, or it will go on thriving until Gabriel's trumpet summons the people to another world."

"Well," said the other speaker, "I am glad to know you believed in Dave Harkins, because I rather liked the man myself."

"I believed in him as I believe in my life."

"What do you think of the son?" asked Bingham, after a short pause.

"Why," said Peterson in his nasal voice; "I kind o' think he's a chip off the old block. I think if he gets a chance he will make good."

"So do I," assented Bingham in a hearty voice.

Herbert, seated behind the partition, could stand the strain no longer. He jumped from his chair and opening the door suddenly, presented himself to the two men. Their astonishment made them speechless. Herbert going over to them, put out his two hands and grasping their hardened palms, he said:

"I have been an unintentional listener to your conversation. I have heard all that you have said about my father and myself, and I want to tell you that I am grateful for the belief you have expressed in his honesty and mine."

"Don't mention it," mumbled Peterson. "I never dreamt you were near by, or I'd been more cautious in my conversation."

"I am glad I heard it," replied Herbert, with glistening eyes. "It has uncovered the truth for me. I have had an offer from New York. I hesitated about leaving Cleverly. I like the Banner, and I like the place; but I find now that my duty is elsewhere. The man who gave that money to my father left here and went straight to New York. He has been swallowed up amid millions of other men; but I'll find him somewhere and in some way if it takes the rest of my life. I thank you, gentlemen, for the things you have said. Before I heard them I was in doubt; now everything is clear to me. My decision is made; I am off to New York."

With flushed face and eager step the young man hurried from the post office and walked rapidly down the main street. Mr. Brooks was preparing to go to his lunch when Herbert hurried into the Banner office.

"I'll see you in about an hour, Herbert," he said smilingly.

"If you will wait a moment I would like to speak to you now," replied Herbert quickly.

"What is it?" asked the other, with an anxious look in his face. "If it's about New York I'd like to tell you that you can take your own time in coming to a decision. Take a week if you need it."

"I don't need a minute," replied Herbert impetuously, "I am grateful to you for your kindness; but my decision is already made. I am going to New York, and I am going at the earliest possible moment."

Mr. Brooks expressed the regret that he felt and then left the young man. Herbert's next task was to inform his mother of his decision. He knew that the change would be a violent one for her, but felt in his heart that he was only doing his duty to her as well as to the memory of his dead father. He walked slowly to his home, and when he entered, found his mother seated in an armchair by the window engaged in some knitting. He walked into the room on tiptoe, and going back of her, threw his arms about her neck.

"Mother," he said softly.

"Well, Herbert," she replied, in a gentle voice. "What is it?"

"I am going to tell you something that may not be pleasant for you to hear, and I want you to promise me that you will bear with it for my sake."

"What is it?" she asked, with a look of pain on her face.

"Will you promise?" he persisted.

"Yes," she said, very slowly, but with emphasis. "I'll promise to be reconciled to anything that is for your good."

"Well," he said after a short pause, "I have come to a decision. I am going to New York, and I am going within forty-eight hours."

The tears came to her eyes, but she bravely repressed them, and arising, took Herbert in her arms and gave him a motherly kiss.

"Bless you, my son," she said, "and go ahead and do what you believe is for the best."

From that time until the moment of his departure Herbert was kept busy in completing his arrangements for moving to the metropolis. His chief business was in completing his work for the current issue of the Banner. When the other persons who were connected with the paper heard of his prospective departure they were very much disappointed because Herbert was a general favorite in the office. The young man himself was so agitated at the thought of leaving those with whom he had been in contact so long and so pleasantly that he could scarcely get through with his routine work.

The morning for his departure dawned at last, and he started for the train with a gripsack in one hand and an umbrella in the other. His mother accompanied him, and on the way gave him a great deal of homely advice regarding his future life in the big city. It was understood that he should go on with his work and if it should prove successful that later on he would send for his mother and thereafter both of them would make their home in New York. In the meantime he promised to send her part of his earnings every week, and in spite of her protests, made the amount the major part of his salary. On the way to the train they passed the home of John Black. Mary Black was just coming out of the doorway, and when she saw the mother and son, joined them on the way to the station.

"I wish you God-speed, Herbert," she said, with undoubted sincerity; "and if you see anything of Arthur it will be a real charity for you to inform us of the fact. Mother and father are very much distressed over his absence."

"Haven't you heard anything from him since he left?" asked Herbert.

"Yes," she replied, holding her head down. "He has written to me twice, each time to ask me for money."

"And you gave it to him?" inquired Herbert.

"Yes," she replied. "Perhaps it was wrong; but I could not refuse it. He did not give any address, but had the mail sent to the General Delivery window of the main post office building."

"Well, Mary," said Herbert, "I assure you that if I am ever in a position to assist you either in Arthur's case, or in any other manner, I will be only too glad to do so."

They had reached the station by this time, and in a moment or two were joined by Noah Brooks, who insisted on coming along to say good-by to his much valued assistant and associate editor.

Brooks was silent for some time, but his face showed the feeling that he was endeavoring to repress. Going over to Herbert, he put his arm around his shoulder in an affectionate manner, and said:

"My boy, I have to thank you for the fidelity you have always shown to my interests. I don't know what in the world I'll do without you; indeed I don't."

Just then the train pulled in at the station and Herbert, after a last good-by, jumped aboard. The engine pulled out quickly, and the young man standing on the rear platform, shook his handkerchief in farewell to his mother and friends. As the train gradually put distance between itself and Cleverly, Herbert was filled with a strange emotion which he could not understand. He was leaving the home of his birth and his youth, and his heart was strangely touched at the thought. The train puffed on, and soon the little group on the station became mere specks in the distance; but the last thing that Herbert saw was the trim figure and the two bright eyes, half dimmed with tears, belonging to Mary Black.

CHAPTER XI
HERBERT IS AWED AND AMAZED BY HIS FIRST SIGHT OF A GREAT CITY

The train made good time, and in two hours arrived in Jersey City. From the shed to the two story ferry-boat which plied between the two shores was but a step. When the boat pulled out into the stream, Herbert was dazzled by the sight that met his eyes. Through force of circumstances over which he had no control, he had never visited New York, and so it came about that this was to be his first view of the wonderful city of the Western Continent. His gaze rested first on the magnificent Statue of Liberty enlightening the world—that colossal bit of statuary placed in New York harbor not only to typify the grandeur of American institutions, but also to emphasize the long friendship existing between America and France. Beyond this he beheld that great piece of engineering known as the Brooklyn Bridge, the girdle, the connecting link which is the visible bond uniting the two great cities of Greater New York.

In the harbor boats were coming and going in every direction, carrying people and merchandise from the four corners of the earth. A monster ocean steamer plowing its way majestically through the waves, its deck literally black with people eager for the first glimpse of land, was making towards the new Castle Garden, there to empty upon the shores of America more men and women than there were in the entire population of Cleverly. Another magnificent ocean greyhound just going down the bay was filled with rich Americans, millionaires and men made suddenly rich who were embarking for foreign shores to spend the money they had dug from the bowels of the earth, or cleverly obtained by ingenuity or trade from their fellow countrymen.

Herbert felt as he gazed out on this constantly moving panorama, as if the whole world had suddenly burst on his view. From the time he left the Jersey City shore until he reached the New York side, his mind was in a whirl trying to grasp and comprehend all the strange sights that were constantly coming within his view. No time was lost in landing, and in a minute or two the country-reared boy found himself in the midst of what seemed to be a hopeless confusion of trucks and drays and cursing drivers. A policeman with uplifted club soon straightened out this tangle, and Herbert proceeded on his way up Cortlandt Street. The rush and roar of the elevated trains, the shouts and protests of the wagon drivers, the yells of the cabmen and peddlers, and the never ceasing hum of talk from the hurrying pedestrians, made Herbert feel as if this were all some wonderful dream.

He spoke to a policeman, asking him the way to Broadway.

"Follow your nose, Johnny, for two blocks," was the flippant rejoinder.

Herbert flushed up a little at this. He was not accustomed to being addressed in such a manner. In fact before he left Cleverly he was looked upon as one of the important persons of the town; but in New York, like many other persons of greater importance, Herbert was soon stripped of his dignity and self-esteem. He continued on his way up the hilly street until he finally found himself on a corner of that throbbing, pulsating, crowded and ever changing thoroughfare which is known by reputation all over the civilized world as Broadway. He walked along its diagonal length for some distance looking in the shop windows, gazing at the crowds, and greedily drinking in the sights that presented themselves on all sides. The noise and the hum and the din were continuous. It began to give him a headache. He wondered how the people were able to stand such a tumultuous existence. Still more, he wondered how soon he would become accustomed to this new condition of things, little thinking that most of that confused multitude had come to New York like himself, a stranger in a strange city, and many of them strangers in a strange land.

After he had partially satisfied his curiosity he determined to look for lodgings. He had the address of Mr. Anderson on a little card. He knew from a letter he had received that it was somewhere on upper Sixth Avenue, and after making one or two mistakes in the direction he took, he finally succeeded in boarding a Sixth Avenue elevated train and was whizzed along towards the up-town section of New York City. It was quite a sensation to ride so far up in the air and to be able to look into the open bedroom windows of the people who lived on either side of the elevated road. He thought he must have surely struck New York on wash-day, because every window and every areaway appeared to be filled with shirts and other articles of wearing apparel. Finally he reached the street that was nearest his destination, and getting out of the train, walked down the high steps towards that section of Sixth Avenue which had been described to him by his former teacher.

On the way, for the first time it dawned upon him that his appearance must be a little bit odd to the pedestrians who passed him on the street. He was twenty-one years old, tall, slender, pale and plain, with twenty-five dollars in his pocket—he had persisted in giving his mother the remainder of his money, claiming that with a position assured he had no need of a large surplus. Nearly all of the clothing he possessed was on his back, and in addition to that his total capital was a knowledge of so much of the art of printing and so much of the art of reporting and editing as a youth is enabled to learn in the office of an enterprising country newspaper. But the most acute feeling that came over him at this time was a sense of terrible loneliness. With the possible exception of Mr. Anderson, he knew no human being within two hundred miles, and his rustic manner and address, he felt satisfied, did not favor the immediate making of new friendships. His personal estate, which was neatly tied up in a little packet, did not encumber him, and he stepped along lightly in his search for Mr. Anderson's boarding house. The landlady proved to be a very pleasant woman, and when he inquired for his friend, told him that he had been unexpectedly called out of the city and would be gone for a week. When he inquired about accommodations she showed him a nice, pleasant room which he could have with board for the sum of $8 a week. Herbert immediately rejected this proffer as being a little more expensive than he was able to undertake.

Somewhat disappointed, he boarded the elevated train once more and was soon whirled down-town. He wandered about aimlessly for some time, wondering where he should look for a boarding house. Passing one of the newspaper offices, he purchased an evening edition and looked in the columns marked "Boarding" and "Rooms to Rent." There were hundreds of advertisements, but they gave no clue to the character of the houses, and very few of them announced their terms. He threw the paper away as useless and continued walking towards the North River. Finally he came to a rather respectable looking house with a brick front, containing the sign "Boarding." He entered, introduced himself to the landlady, and was offered shelter and subsistence at $5 a week. The room that was offered for his inspection was comfortable, and the price seemed reasonable, so he closed the bargain at once.

After depositing his little package in his room and washing himself and ridding his clothing of the stains of travel, he left the house to make some purchases of little articles that were necessary for his attire. Once again he walked about in a rather aimless manner, and in the course of his travels finally reached the thoroughfare known as the Bowery. It proved to be quite a different place from the street that he had pictured in his mind. There were some few dance halls and concert rooms, it is true, but in addition to that he was surprised to see the unusually large number of bright looking retail stores and business houses. He was gazing in the window of one of these stores when someone tapped him on the arm and said in a whining voice:

"Say, boss, can't you help a poor fellow out?"

He turned quickly, and to his great astonishment, beheld Harry Adler standing before him. He had not seen the man since he left Cleverly in company with Arthur Black. The appearance of Adler indicated that he had been a victim either of great misfortune, or of the persistent laziness which seemed to be part of his character. He was very thinly clad; in fact his coat seemed to be a mass of rags, and there were holes in the rough shoes that he wore on his feet. A hat with a torn brim covered his bushy hair, and he was entirely innocent of collar or necktie. A heavy beard suggested continuous neglect of the barber.

"Harry Adler!" exclaimed Herbert. "You are the last man in the world I expected to meet."

"Yes, I guess that's so," said Adler, beginning to sniffle; "but you see, Herbert, I've been playing in very hard luck. I came to the city to get work, and after I had been at it for about a week I was taken sick and sent to the hospital. When I came out of that institution I was so weak that I was not able to hunt for employment, and I finally got in such a condition that I had to beg for a bit to eat."

Herbert looked at the fellow in a skeptical manner. Then he gave a significant sniff of his nose.

"I guess you've been drinking," he cried. "Probably that has prevented you from being a successful business man in New York."

Adler pretended not to notice this bit of irony and continued:

"Herbert, you've got a chance to make a man out of me. I know we haven't been very good friends; but if you will help to straighten me out you will never have cause to regret it."

"Where is Arthur Black?" asked Herbert, disregarding the other's appeal.

"He's up at my boarding house," replied Adler, with a whimper.

"Well, I would like to see him very much," responded Herbert. "Will you promise to make an arrangement so that I can meet him somewhere to-night?"

"Yes, indeed I will," replied the other, "if you will help me out a little bit I will do anything for you."

"Well I don't want you to do anything, except to have Arthur Black meet me."

"All right; I'll do that."

"Where is your boarding house?" asked Herbert.

Adler looked a little bit scared at this question, and then said in a husky tone:

"Oh, it wouldn't do for you to come to our boarding house. It's too humble for the likes of you; but I tell you what I'll do. I'll arrange to have Arthur Black meet you in the corridor of the main post office building at eight o'clock to-night. I'll do that sure if you help me out."

The constant appeal for personal help finally impressed itself upon Herbert, and he said:

"What do you want?"

"Well," said the other in a quavering voice, "I guess a coat and a shave and a pair of shoes wouldn't be bad to start with."

"All right, I'll try to fit you out with them," said Herbert, "if you don't let it cost too much."

So the queerly assorted pair entered a clothing house on the Bowery, where Adler succeeded in obtaining a coat and a pair of shoes for ten dollars. Following that he was taken into a barber shop and treated to a clean shave and haircut. The improvement in his appearance was remarkable.

"How do you feel now?" asked Herbert, looking at him approvingly.

"Pretty good, but mighty hungry."

"Well, come with me, and I'll get you something to eat."

The two men repaired to a near-by restaurant and Adler was treated to what was probably the best meal he had enjoyed in many a long day.

Herbert settled the score, and once more telling him to be sure to have Arthur Black at the post office at eight o'clock, parted with him and went around to his own lodgings. He looked over his money and found that after paying his board and spending money for food and clothing on Adler and giving the lazy one a two dollar bill, he had only four dollars left to his credit. He was somewhat annoyed at this; but consoled himself with the thought that he would begin employment the next day and would soon have sufficient ready money to satisfy all of his needs. At times he felt angry with himself for having helped Adler, who after all that was said and done, was a very worthless sort of fellow. But on reflection he felt that he might have done the man some good, and that thought was sufficient to give him a feeling of pleasant self-satisfaction.

He left the house immediately after dinner, and after a short walk on Broadway, found himself in the corridor of the main post office at a quarter before eight. He stationed himself in such a position as to command a view of all of those who entered or left the building. It was irksome business waiting for anyone in that place. The hands of the clock gradually moved around and it finally struck eight, but there was no sign of Arthur Black. Herbert waited on, feeling that the expected visitor would be likely to come in at any minute; but time continued to pass, and finally the clock struck nine. Herbert turned and left the building, filled with great disgust:

"Buncoed!" he muttered to himself. "Buncoed, by gosh! My first day in New York and I permit myself to be buncoed by a man who was even without standing in Cleverly! That's a pretty good lesson for my first day in the metropolis."

CHAPTER XII
IN WHICH HERBERT BECOMES ACQUAINTED WITH SOME OF THE METHODS OF MODERN JOURNALISM

Herbert had been advised to call at the Argus office at noon for the purpose of presenting his letter of introduction to Mr. Blakeley, the city editor of that newspaper. He prepared himself carefully for the forthcoming interview, trying especially in a half conscious way to rid himself of the rustic appearance which he felt might lessen his prospects, or impair his prestige with the newspaper man he was about to meet. The Argus office was located almost in the center of the cluster of large buildings on Park Row, and as Herbert looked up at the edifice he could not repress a feeling of pride at the thought that in a day or so he would be numbered among the busy workers in that bee-hive of industry.

He took the elevator and was shot up to the fifth floor with a suddenness that almost took his breath away. A boy standing at the door of this landing demanded his card, and while Herbert sat there waiting for a reply he noticed that the door was kept locked, and that newcomers were greeted with a large sign which read:

"Positively no admittance except on business."

He thought this was rather inhospitable at the time, but later in his career realized that it was a necessity in order to permit the orderly and speedy transaction of business. A newspaper office is looked upon as the Mecca for eccentric people of all kinds and characters and if they were admitted promiscuously they would consume the time of the editors and reporters and make it impossible to issue the paper at all.

Presently the office boy returned, and said:

"Step inside."

He walked into a large room and was directed to a smaller room, which was partitioned off in the extreme corner. A tall, thin man rose to greet him, and nodding in a friendly way, pointed to a chair:

"I am sorry," said this gentleman, "that Mr. Blakeley, the city editor of the Argus, is not here to-day. This is his day off. However he spoke to me about you and I am very glad to meet you; but it is not possible for me to serve you in any way to-day. It will be necessary for you to see him in person before you can go to work."

Herbert thanked him for his courtesy and the pleasant manner in which he had been greeted and promised to return again the next day. In the few minutes he was in the office he noticed that the room was gradually beginning to assume an air of activity. Men were coming in constantly and seating themselves in front of desks in the large apartment, which because of the ink and paper and pencils and furniture looked very much like a large edition of the old schoolroom in Cleverly.

Herbert was quite disappointed at not seeing Mr. Blakeley on his first visit, but resolved to utilize the remainder of the day by sight-seeing. He visited many of the places of interest in New York, including the Aquarium, the tomb of General Grant at Riverside Park, and the Metropolitan Museum in Central Park. All of these things were deeply interesting, and in a larger sense highly educational. On his way home he purchased copies of all the afternoon papers, and after dinner that evening spent several hours in going over them very carefully with a view of becoming familiar with the style of reporting that prevailed on the popular newspapers in New York City. In spite of the fact that he had put in a very busy day he went to bed with a feeling of regret over the apparent loss of two whole days.

At noon the following day he was again at the Argus office, and this time was successful in meeting Mr. Blakeley. The city editor was a short, stockily built man, wearing eyeglasses and possessed of a quick, nervous manner. He looked Herbert over from head to foot as soon as he entered and gazed at him very earnestly during all the course of their brief conversation.

"Harkins," he said, after the usual greeting, "I am going to put you on the Argus at a salary. This is somewhat unusual, because nearly all on our staff are space men. New men especially are put on space, which simply means that they are paid for what they write, in order to test their ability. But Mr. Anderson, who is an old friend of mine, has recommended you so highly that I am going to put you on the regular staff at once; and I will give you three weeks in which to demonstrate your ability to hold the place down permanently."

"I thank you very much," said Herbert, "I will try to prove myself worthy of the confidence you are placing in me."

"That's all right," said the other skeptically, "I don't want any promises; all I want is the performance."

"All right, sir," said Herbert; "I'll not make any promises; but I can assure you that I will try to size up to the position."

"That sounds business," retorted the other in his quick, jerky style. Then looking up at the calendar, he said musingly: "It's a little too late in the week for you to do anything now. You can report for duty at noon next Monday. Meantime I would advise you to become acquainted with the city and its institutions, and to book yourself up as speedily as possible on the men and things who go to make up life in this busy town."

Herbert promised to do as he was advised, and then met the tall, spare man with whom he had held the conversation the day before. This was the assistant city editor, who took him in hand and introduced him to such other members of the Argus staff as were in the office at that time. They were all pleasant and affable, but Herbert took an immediate and special liking to Francis Tomlin, one of the reporters, who had greeted him in a very kindly spirit.

"Don't permit the noise and bustle and confusion of this place to confuse you," said Tomlin, "because it will not take you many days to know that that is merely the outer covering, or what we might call the atmosphere of the place. You will find that the work itself moves along in a precise and systematic manner. Come in to-night around the midnight hour and see the office going at full blast."

Herbert accepted the invitation, and just before the clock towers were striking the mystic hour he entered the local room of the Argus. Tomlin had phrased it correctly. The office was in full blast. The news room immediately adjoined the city room, and between the two the noise and bustle and air of activity were confusing to one not accustomed to that sort of thing. Telegraph instruments in two corners of the room ticked away continuously. A man at the long distance telephone sat in front of a typewriter and transcribed a story that was being sent in over the wire from a little town fifteen miles away. The assistant city editor shouted through the speaking tube to the foreman of the composing room about every ten or fifteen minutes. Telegraph boys came in every few minutes, carrying little yellow envelopes bearing within their modest covers the news of the entire habitable globe. The news editors sitting at their big desks tore the wrappings off these silent messengers, and after editing them, put suggestive and snappy headlines over them for the benefit of their thousands of readers of the following morning. A dozen reporters sitting at their desks scratched away for dear life, or pounded the typewriters in their haste to put the words together which were to furnish the subscribers of the Argus with a comprehensive account of everything of interest that had happened in the great city during the previous twenty-four hours. Nothing was too small, nothing too great to be gathered in this enormous dragnet of publicity and furnished to eager men and women with their coffee and rolls on the following morning.

Herbert was entranced with the scene. He had already been fascinated by the smell of printers' ink and had a very intelligent idea of the methods of modern journalism; but this scene wherein apparently hopeless confusion gradually worked itself out into perfect order and system, furnished the capstone to his already stimulated imagination. He longed to take an active part in it.

As he looked around the room his eye was attracted to little slips of paper posted on a bulletin board near the city editor's desk. These informed all who were interested, whether John Jones or John Smith was absent or on duty; prohibited the men from smoking in the office, and contained little bits of poetry and anecdotes which had been surreptitiously posted there by some of the men on the staff. There was one thing on the bulletin board that attracted Herbert's attention more than anything else. It might be called a code of fundamental principles for the aspiring reporter. It read as follows:

"Be accurate, courteous, earnest, enterprising, enthusiastic, faithful, honest, manly, modest, observant, persevering, pleasant, prompt, quick, sensible, shrewd, tactful, temperate.

"Ask plenty of questions, and don't forget the answers.

"Know all you can, but don't know it all.

"Study history, political economy, learn shorthand, use a typewriter.

"Keep posted on current events; cultivate numerous acquaintances; say little, listen much.

"Never violate confidence; be honest with yourself, your employers, and the public. Have a conscience. Don't fake. Merit confidence. Command respect.

"Know men; know facts, then write the plain truth simply. Write plainly and avoid flub. Write for the people. Write English. Be clear, concise, direct.

"When sent for news get it, and get it right. Accuracy, accuracy, accuracy.

"Never write anything you would not sign your name to. Realize your responsibility.

"Never be unjust or unmanly; cultivate a pleasant address, be persistent, but polite.

"Observe everything. Study human nature. Study newspapers of different cities and make a model of the best.

"Cultivate humor. Be charitable. Speak kindly.

"Keep your presence of mind.

"Read good literature; avoid debasing associations.

"Hustle."

After reading this, and resolving to memorize it for his own benefit, Herbert went to one of the unoccupied desks and began looking over some of the newspapers. While he was thus engaged the assistant city editor rushed up to him carrying a clipping taken from one of the afternoon papers.

"See here, Harkins!" he shouted, "how would you like to make yourself useful—you're not on the staff yet, but it won't do you any harm to try and get your hand in."

"I'd be delighted," said Herbert; "what is it?"

"Here, take this clipping," was the reply; "it's from one of the afternoon papers. I'd like you to re-write it and condense it for the Argus. Get it up quickly. It's for one of the inside pages, and it must be in the composing room before one o'clock."

Herbert took the clipping and read it carefully. It told about the arrival in New York of Madame Bonneville, a celebrated French actress, who was coming to this country for the purpose of making her farewell tour. There was a spirited description of her arrival on the pier amid a cloud of trunks, packages and dress-suit cases, not to mention two or three bird cages, half a dozen umbrellas, a green poll-parrot and a pet poodle dog which she insisted on carrying in her arms and embracing in a most motherly fashion.

Herbert gazed at this account long and earnestly. It contained a brief interview with the actress, and while the whole thing was intensely interesting and human, it really contained little actual news excepting the fact that the actress had arrived and being wearied with her long journey, had retired immediately to her apartments. How to re-write and reduce this article and make it different from the clipping, and yet retain the news and the interest, was the problem that presented itself to the young aspirant for journalistic honors. He got down to work at last, however, because he felt that if a person intended doing a thing there was nothing like doing it. It would not be wise to theorize much while the assistant city editor was shouting for copy. Herbert never worked harder on any of the things he had contributed to his own little paper in the country than he did on the re-writing of this scrap of New York news. After much patient labor, he finally completed his work, and found to his satisfaction that he had reduced the article just one-half and still retained some semblance of a good story. He carried it over to the assistant city editor, who glanced at it hastily, and said sharply, without the slightest note of explanation:

"Won't do. Too long. Put it in a stick or two."

Herbert walked back to his desk rather disappointed. He knew that the news in the article could be put into a stick or two, but he felt instinctively that the item would be robbed of all its interest. However, he sat down once more and wrote a ten line paragraph, which met with the approval and acceptance of the busy assistant city editor.

He arose early the next morning and hunted for a copy of the Argus with much eagerness. He knew that the little paragraph which he had finally turned in at his first piece of work in New York did not amount to anything; but he could not restrain the longing desire to see himself in print for the first time in a metropolitan newspaper. He took the Argus and went over it with extreme care from the first to the last page. Nothing in the paper escaped his keen, inquiring gaze. When he had concluded he laid it aside with a sigh of disappointment.

His ten line story had not been printed.

CHAPTER XIII
HERBERT MAKES A HIT AND TIDES OVER A TEMPORARY FINANCIAL DIFFICULTY

Herbert was still young enough to be sensitive, and the thought that his maiden effort in the big city had probably found its way into the waste paper basket was galling to his natural pride. However, he braced himself and called at the office at noon again, and smilingly greeted his colleagues. He learned some things during the day, and one was a conviction that success on a country newspaper did not necessarily fit a man for immediate employment on a metropolitan daily. He had a long and confidential talk with Frank Tomlin, during the course of which he related his experience and the fate of his first item.

Tomlin laughed heartily at the recital.

"You can't afford to be thin-skinned in New York, my boy," he replied. "Besides, you are mistaken about your item. It was written all right, but was crowded out in the make-up."

"Do you think so?"

"I am satisfied of it. I have helped Blakeley to make up the paper on more than one occasion, and there were times when stories bigger and more important than yours and which were in type were thrown aside for want of space. So don't let a little thing like that trouble you. Persevere; do the best you can, and don't permit yourself to be cast down by little incidents of this kind."

Herbert thanked him for this friendly advice and promised to profit by it. The talk caused Tomlin to drift into a train of reminiscences.

"I'll never forget my first experience in the newspaper business in this city," he said musingly; "it satisfied me that enterprise, while quite valuable in itself, is not the most important thing in the gathering of news. I know that when I began I was eager to accomplish great things.

"One morning the city editor assigned me to a meeting of the Municipal League, and as I was leaving the room he called out:

"'See here, I want you to put a little ginger in your articles. We want to brighten the paper up a bit.'

"It was a prosy gathering. Most of the members of the league were elderly or old men, and they made long winded speeches and accomplished little business. There did not seem to be much prospect of a bright article in the ordinary report of a meeting of this character. I decided to burlesque the meeting. The result was all that could be desired. The city editor was not 'on' and the story went straight to the copy desk.

"The next morning I was informed the proprietor wanted to see me. I felt at once that this summons had something to do with my article. When I entered the room, he looked at me curiously and in silence for some moments.

"'Did you write the meeting of the Municipal League which appears in this morning's paper?'

"'I did,' I answered, swelling up with pride.

"He was silent.

"'Didn't you like the report?' I finally inquired.

"'Yes,' he said, prolonging the word in a strange manner.

"'Wasn't it good enough?' I inquired.

"'Oh, yes,' with a peculiar laugh; 'it was bright.' Then turning to me he said impressively: 'I have no doubt in the world that the members of the league deserve all the ridicule you cast on them, but,' he added, 'it should not have been printed in my paper. I am the president of the Municipal League.'"

Herbert and Tomlin remained in conversation for a long while, and the older man regaled his companion with a batch of very interesting stories bearing upon the incidents that take place behind the scenes of journalism. They walked home together that night, and Herbert, feeling that Tomlin was a man in whom he could trust and confide, confessed to him the low condition of his finances.

"I thought I would get immediate employment," he said, "and as a consequence brought only a small amount of money with me from the country. I met an old acquaintance who was on his uppers and gave him a large part of my surplus. As the result of this and my other little expenditures, I have only about two dollars."

"Do you want to borrow anything?" said the other, turning to him quickly; "I will be glad to stake you if you do."

"Not at all," said Herbert hastily, "I hope you won't think I introduced the subject for that purpose. But it will be about ten days before I receive my first pay; and in the meantime next week's board bill will be due and payable. I wondered whether I could not earn a little money in the meantime."

"Certainly," said Tomlin; "it will give you an opportunity for showing what is in you, too. The thing is easy enough. Write some space for the Argus. Blakeley is always willing to accept a good story, and if you can go out into this human whirlpool to-morrow and fish up something a little bit out of the ordinary he will be only too glad to print it, and pay you for it, too."

The following day, acting on the suggestion of his friend, Herbert made the rounds of the city hospitals. The usual routine stories presented themselves at all of these institutions; but most of them were covered by staff men, and for that reason were not available for a special space-writer. While Herbert was pondering over what was best to do under the circumstances, it suddenly dawned on him that perhaps the obvious thing might make the best story after all. Things that were happening every day in the week were looked upon as being trite and trivial. If he could take one of these incidents and lift it out of the rut and make it stand toweringly above other incidents of a like character he would make a hit. To think was to act. He went to the head keeper in the next hospital and asked to look over the book of records. Among the items inscribed there was one which told about a patient who had attempted suicide, but whose life would be saved. Herbert asked whether he could obtain the details of this story, and was told that if he applied to one of the assistants in the main ward he might obtain some additional information. He did obtain more facts, and he hurried to the office, eager to write the story. The heading was "How a Trained Nurse Defeated Death."

The introduction described how a demure little nurse in the hospital who looked as if she might weigh not more than one hundred pounds, started on a walking match against death at five o'clock in the evening, and finished at six o'clock in the morning—a winner. The story went on and told how the ambulance had brought a twenty-two year old girl to the hospital after she had swallowed enough opium to send three or four strong men to their death. The poor, misguided girl who had taken the poison on account of a case of unrequited love, showed a strong desire to go to sleep. The little nurse knew that if the girl closed her eyes they would never again open in this world; so she tried to keep her awake by slapping her on the back.

That method was not strenuous enough, so the long walk was started. It was up and down the corridor of the receiving ward, and out into the hall and the yard. Whenever the nurse became tired she sat down to rest for a moment; but as soon as the girl nodded the walk was resumed. All through the lonesome hours of the night this unique feat of pedestrianism was continued. Daylight appeared, and still the walk went on. Finally the clock struck six, and the two women were still walking. Shortly after that the house physician made his appearance, and giving the girl a careful examination, pronounced her out of danger. Then, and not until then, the nurse went to sleep, and even while Herbert was writing his picturesque story she was still sleeping the sleep of the just and the brave.

His story made over a column in the Argus. It proved to be a palpable hit. Blakeley, the city editor, who did not see it until he picked up the paper the next morning, gloated over it with the glee with which a miser examines a newly found diamond. He patted Herbert on the back and said that if he continued to turn in stories of that character his period of probation would be short indeed and his permanence on the paper assured.

But the best feature of the incident, to Herbert's mind, came on Friday afternoon, when he called at the business office and received a check for $8 for his piece of special reporting. This gave him a total cash balance of $10 and enabled him to pay his board bill and to look forward with confidence to the coming of his regular pay-days.

CHAPTER XIV
IN WHICH HERBERT IS GIVEN AN UNUSUAL
OPPORTUNITY TO DISTINGUISH HIMSELF

After he had been on the Argus for about a month, Herbert felt entirely at home. He managed to get along very smoothly with all the members of the staff. Blakeley, the city editor, was especially pleased with the new addition to his local force. He found that he was punctual, industrious and anxious to do his work to the very best of his ability. The other reporters at the same time looked on him as an agreeable fellow who was willing to do them a good turn whenever he had the chance to do so. At the end of his second month on the paper he was gratified at the receipt of an unsolicited increase in his salary. His particular friend on the Argus, Francis Tomlin, obtained a promotion at the same time; and the two young men put their heads together and decided to seek a pleasant room near the office. After a search that consumed nearly all the idle hours of a whole week, they finally obtained an apartment which had the added advantage of a neat and well kept bath-room. Herbert lost no time in removing his effects from the modest quarters which he had occupied since his first arrival in New York. The two young men were together very much, and the fact that they were employed at night and had many hours of leisure during the day gave them the chance of strolling about the city or seeking amusements together at a time when most other men were busily engaged in their trades and professions.

The new room, which was comfortably furnished in the first place, rapidly grew more habitable through the skill and good taste of the two reporters. The gift of a set of books from home first gave Herbert the idea of accumulating a library. Tomlin joined with him, and in a surprisingly short time they were the possessors of quite a valuable little library which counted among its principal assets several important books of reference.

One day Herbert was delighted to receive a visit from Mr. Anderson, who had been his school-teacher for so many years in Cleverly. In honor of the event he begged off from the office for the night, and secured a similar privilege for Tomlin. The three men sat in the room till long past midnight, chatting about books and newspapers and other topics of a congenial nature. Mr. Anderson told the story of "barring out day" at the school in Cleverly, and the recital was done so well that it filled Tomlin with delight and caused him to laugh with such heartiness that the tears fairly ran down his cheeks.

On another occasion a little later in the year Noah Brooks, the editor of the Cleverly Banner, visited New York, and while in the city was the guest of Herbert Harkins. The young man was very much pleased at the thought of entertaining the veteran editor, who had been such a good friend to him in

Cleverly. He took Tomlin into his confidence, and between them they planned a program which kept Mr. Brooks engaged every minute of the day and night during his four days' stay in the metropolis. In fact Herbert exhausted his resources in showing the visitor what he was pleased to call "the time of his life." As the three men walked along Broadway together, Mr. Brooks looking up at the high buildings on either side of him, said musingly:

"Herbert, it's been over forty years since I visited this town before, and I want to say that there have been many changes since then."

"I should say so," replied Herbert, with a laugh; "in fact, although I have been here only a few months I can see changes that are going on at the present time."

"Yes, many changes," assented the old editor, nodding his head in a reflective manner; "and these changes are not only in the big buildings, but in the big men. I may be mistaken, but I don't think you produce the kind of men that we had in the days when I was in my prime. However, I won't insist on that. It may simply be the natural thought of every old man."

"Who would you regard as the most conspicuous man that was here when you visited the city last?" asked Herbert, anxious to draw upon his friend's inexhaustible fund of recollections.

"Well," he replied, "that's a pretty hard question to answer after all these years; but I think that perhaps good old Horace Greeley was the best of them all. When I was here last I met him in the flesh. Now all that you have of him is that statue in front of the Tribune Building and the memory of his honest, old fashioned life."

The old gentleman sighed at this as if he were not quite sure that the good old times would ever come again. Indeed he was a type of man very similar to the famous editor, whom he was accustomed to look upon as the greatest man of his day and generation. Mr. Brooks was careless in his dress, quaint in his manner and unyielding in his integrity. Tomlin enjoyed the visit of the country editor, if anything, more than Herbert; and he was really sorry when the trip came to an end, and he went with Herbert to the depot to bid good-by to the whole-souled old man.

In the meantime Herbert continued to make satisfactory progress in the Argus office. He was receiving all kinds of assignments now, and he soon had the reputation of being a man who did his work perfectly. More than this, he was marked down as a reliable reporter, which is a very important thing on any newspaper. The city editor felt that when an assignment was placed in his hand it was sure to be covered and the copy turned in at the earliest possible moment. One morning as they were leaving the house together, Tomlin said to Herbert:

"Some day, old man, you will get a very big thing to do, and it may be the means of either making or breaking you."

The occasion came sooner than expected. That very morning the city editor summoned Herbert to his private office, and said:

"See here, Harkins, I am going to give you a chance to show what there is in you. I have here what I regard as a very delicate and difficult piece of work. It requires perseverance, and I am willing to give you the job if you will tell me that you will stick at it and never quit until your efforts have been crowned with success. Can you give me that promise?"

Herbert smiled at this vigorous presentation of the case, and said:

"Well, Mr. Blakeley, if it is a piece of newspaper work that comes within my ability, I feel reasonably sure of coming out successful."

"Well," said the other, in his short, snappy tones, "here is a letter. It's a small clue as a starting point. Read it over, and then come back to me."

Herbert went to his desk and read the letter as directed. It was from a poor woman who had been induced to send $2 of her hard earned money to a concern which promised to teach her how to paint on china within two weeks, and after that time to furnish her with steady employment which would pay her anywhere from $10 to $20 a week, according to her speed and ability. She said in her letter that she had sent the money, and in return received a flimsy circular which gave some crude and utterly impracticable directions of how to paint. The thing was worthless to her and her $2 wasted.

When Herbert had finished reading this, he returned to Blakeley and said:

"Have you any further directions?"

"No," was the reply, "you will have to work on your own resources from now on. I suppose that eventually the postal authorities will hear of this swindle and refuse to permit this sort of thing to go through the mails; but in the meantime we know about it and we want to get the credit of stopping it at once. You take the address of this woman and go ahead and see what you can make of it."

Herbert called upon the woman that afternoon, and in less than an hour had obtained a very good story from her, backed up by a sworn statement of her experience with the concern. At the same time he learned the names and addresses of ten other persons who had been swindled in a similar manner.

Altogether four days were consumed in visiting and interviewing these persons. Some of them who had natural ability, had learned to paint on china in spite of the bungling directions sent out by the concern; but when they wrote to the company and asked for the employment that was to pay them from $10 to $20 a week their letters were ignored. Altogether the young reporter had what might be called a first class story. When he had all of his facts in good shape he went to the city editor again, and said:

"Mr. Blakeley, I want you to give me authority to employ a private detective. I have everything in perfect condition at present, and all I need is the climax, which I hope to bring about at noon to-morrow. In other words, it is necessary to arrest someone connected with this concern. If we do this, I will have plenty of witnesses, and we can have the scoundrel held for court."

"Capital! Capital!" shouted Blakeley. "I will give you the authority to employ a detective at once. How do you propose going about it?"

"That is quite simple," answered Herbert; "the company has a box in the post office. I have sent a decoy letter, which should be placed in the box between eleven and twelve o'clock to-morrow. They probably employ a go-between, or a messenger, who gathers up the letters and takes them to the head swindler. We must arrest this person, whoever he is, and probably with a little ingenuity we may be able to extort a confession from him, and then go after the other fellows. In the meantime I am going back to my room and will start to typewrite the story. I have it blocked out, so that we can make a full page scare out of it. We ought to have a picture of the man who comes after the letters, and then, if possible, a photograph of the head swindler, and interviews with all the victims."

Blakeley looked at the young man with admiration written in every line of his countenance. He put out his short, pudgy hand, and slapped Herbert on the back.

"Harkins, you are all right. You'll do. Go ahead, my boy, and I wish you luck in your undertaking."

CHAPTER XV
IN WHICH HERBERT DOES SOME VERY HARD WORK AND RECEIVES A TERRIBLE SHOCK

Herbert arose much earlier than usual the next morning, for he had a keen appreciation of the important character of the work that lay before him. He had hardly finished his breakfast when there was a ring at the door and the landlady brought up a card which bore upon its glazed surface the simple inscription "M. Short." Herbert wondered who this could be, but directed that he be sent up to his room at once. A few minutes later he was greeting a short-set, stockily-built man, with sharp eyes and a sad expression of countenance.

"Well, Mr. Short," said Herbert, "what can I do for you?"

The bright eyes of the little man twinkled merrily as he responded:

"I fear that I will have to put the shoe on the other foot and kindly inquire what I can do for you."

"Why," said Herbert, "I never met you before."

"Probably not," replied the other, still smiling; "but I was ordered to report to you this morning, and told that you would give me directions how to proceed."

"Oh!" exclaimed Herbert, a light breaking in on him, "you are the detective."

"Yes," said the other mildly, "that is my business, and I am now at your service."

After a conversation of ten or fifteen minutes, the reporter and the detective came to a thorough understanding. They were to meet at the main post office shortly before noon, and their movements after that were to depend entirely upon circumstances. Herbert was pleased with the character of man who had been sent to assist him, and mentally congratulated himself upon what now appeared to be the certain success of many days of hard labor. The end was already in view.

A few minutes after the detective had taken his leave, Herbert received a square cornered envelope, containing his name and address. He tore it open quickly and read as follows:

"DEAR HERBERT:

"Father, mother and I have removed to New York for the winter, and would be glad to have you call at the earliest opportunity. We understand that you are engaged in your newspaper work in the evening, so that if you care you are quite welcome to call in the morning, or at any other time that may suit your convenience.

"Very sincerely yours,
"MARY BLACK."

Herbert looked at his watch. He had nearly three hours to spare before it would be time to keep his appointment with the detective in the post office, and he quickly decided to utilize it by making a hurried call on the Blacks. The address given was that of a house on West 69th Street, and in a very short time, by making use of the sub-way, Herbert found himself at the address indicated.

Mary Black, who responded to his call, was delighted to see her old friend and schoolmate, and in a few minutes he was also talking with Mr. and Mrs. Black. The family, distressed by the continued absence of the son and brother, had determined to stay in New York for some months in the hope of obtaining some clue to the runaway. A financial friend of Mr. Black, who had gone to Europe for the winter, had insisted upon his occupancy of the house during the time that he was absent from the country. Although the suggestion had been made only a fortnight before, the little family was already comfortably installed in the 69th Street house. They were all delighted with their new surroundings, and Mary was very much pleased and interested with the sights of the big city; but over it all there was a certain sadness caused by the sorrow which was felt on account of the erring one. The father was almost completely crushed at the domestic affliction which overshadowed their hearthstone. He had lost the coldness and haughtiness for which he was distinguished while at Cleverly, and in broken tones expressed to Herbert the sorrow he felt at the injustice which he had done to his old friend, David Harkins. He said that if an opportunity should ever come whereby he would be enabled to remedy the ill that had been caused through his thoughtless words, he would cheerfully do so.

Time passed so rapidly and so pleasantly in the company of Mary Black that Herbert was loath to leave. A look at his watch, however, showed that he had less than an hour before the time would arrive for keeping his appointment, so he bade good-by to Mr. and Mrs. Black and hurried towards the door. Mary accompanied him there, and he noticed from her constrained manner that she had something on her mind and was anxious to speak to him privately. Being a man, he felt that it was incumbent upon him to break the ice, so he said gently:

"Mary, is there anything I can do for you or your father or mother? If so, don't hesitate to speak to me frankly."

"There is something, Herbert," she said, "and it has been weighing upon my mind for a long while. It is about Arthur. I want you to promise me that you will be a friend to my brother. I do not believe that he is a bad boy at heart; but unfortunately, he has fallen into bad company and has been led astray. Promise me that if the opportunity ever presents itself, you will give him a helping hand. This chance may come, or it may never come; but tell me that you will not forget what I have said to you."

Herbert took her by the hand, and said with much solemnity:

"Mary, if I ever meet Arthur and have the opportunity of befriending him, I promise you that I shall do so."

Her eyelashes were wet with tears; but at his words, her eyes sparkled with satisfaction, and she exclaimed eagerly:

"Oh, I thank you so much for saying that, because I know that I can trust you, and I know that you mean what you say."

A few minutes later Herbert was once more in the sub-way, speeding towards the Park Row station, which was within a short distance of the main post office building. He reached that busy spot at ten minutes of twelve o'clock and found the detective awaiting him. The two men held a hurried interview with the clerk of the box department, who informed them that he knew the young man who was in the habit of calling for the letters for the swindling concern which they now had under suspicion. He said that he would remain at his post for the next fifteen or twenty minutes and as soon as he identified the fellow he would give the two men a signal by holding up his right hand. The details of the plan having been arranged, the reporter and the detective set themselves to wait for the critical moment. It proved to be a great strain on all concerned. The hands of the big clock moved around so slowly that they could almost have shrieked out with impatience and anxiety. A great crowd was hurrying to and fro and opening and closing the letter boxes, which reached almost from the pavement to the ceiling all along the great corridor, but the moments dragged by and the clerk had made no signal.

Presently a man wearing a long ulster and a derby hat stooped down on one knee and began opening the letter box which contained the mail belonging to the china painting concern. He entered so quickly that neither Herbert nor the detective caught a glimpse of his face. The box clerk inside the office became very much excited when the man stooped down, and getting a good look at his face, raised his hand and shook it in the air as a signal to those on the outside. It said just as clearly as if the words had been spoken:

"There is your man. Nab him."

The detective moved to one side so that he could arrest his man the minute he arose from his sitting position. Herbert, who was becoming quite nervous from the strain, motioned the detective to step back a few yards. When this had been done, the young reporter got immediately in the rear of the kneeling man so that when he arose he could face him and make his accusation as dramatically as possible. He felt that this was to be a great occasion in his journalistic life, and he wanted it to come off successfully and without the slightest slip.

The man in the ulster was terribly slow about his work. His head and his face were so close to the box that it was impossible to get a glimpse of his countenance. Besides he fingered each letter separately as if to feel and mentally calculate the amount of money enclosed in each of the envelopes. The action did not escape Herbert's attention, and caused him to curl his lips up in a look of unutterable scorn.

"Calculating his stealings," he muttered to himself indignantly; "considering how much money he has filched from poor girls and women who have scarcely enough to buy food to eat."

The kneeling figure, however, knew nothing of the contempt with which he was being regarded by the warm-blooded young man behind him. Presently he finished his examination of the letters and had put them all in the little leather gripsack which he had beside him. He arose very slowly, and then turned around and came face to face with the young reporter.

The sight that met the gaze of Herbert Harkins caused him to become as pale as a sheet. His head seemed to be reeling around him, and he felt as if he could scarcely stand without support.

He looked again. The second glance only confirmed what he had seen at first.

The youth who stood before him was Arthur Black!

CHAPTER XVI
IN WHICH HERBERT LOSES HIS POSITION AND RETIRES IN DISGRACE

The shock of discovering Arthur Black so unexpectedly and under such damaging circumstances completely unnerved Herbert Harkins. For many seconds he stood there staring at Arthur as if he were some ghostly phantom who had suddenly appeared from the grave. By degrees Herbert began to realize the compromising position in which he had placed himself. The detective stood only a few yards away eagerly watching the scene and awaiting the moment when he would be called upon to place Arthur Black under arrest. Herbert did not turn around, but felt that the sleuth was there, ready to perform the act which was to be the capstone of a remarkably clever piece of newspaper work.

In that brief period of time his mind traveled with lightning like rapidity. He thought of his troubles in the country. He remembered the incident when he had punished Arthur. He recalled the threatened disgrace which had preceded his father's sudden death. He remembered his work on the Cleverly Banner, and then by easy stages his mind reverted to his arrival in New York, his employment on the Argus, and finally to his meeting with Mary Black on that very morning. He thought of Blakeley, the city editor, impatiently waiting for the announcement that his big story was to be a success and that the Argus could pride itself not only upon a notable scoop, but also upon the exposure of a set of swindlers who had preyed remorselessly upon the public.

What should he do? His duty seemed clear and unavoidable. Surely one would have to suffer for the benefit of the many. Besides that the eyes of the detective were upon him, and his failure to do the right thing at this moment might lead to his complete downfall. From this thought his mind reverted to every detail of the impressive interview which he had held with Mary Black a little more than an hour before. A voice within him urged him to be faithful to his promise, no matter what personal loss he might suffer. He had given her his pledge that if he ever met Arthur Black he would lend him a helping hand; that if he was in trouble he would succor him; that if he was in danger he would save him. For what seemed to be a very long time he was torn with conflicting emotions. Many minutes seemed to elapse—in reality it was only a few seconds. He reached his decision quickly, and he acted promptly. Putting his arm on Arthur's shoulder, he whispered, almost hissed, into the latter's ear:

"You are on the verge of ruin. I have been sent here to arrest you. A detective is standing a few yards away. If you wish to avoid arrest, exposure and disgrace, run—run for your life."

Arthur clutched convulsively at the grip in his right hand and gave a hurried look about him. His glance fell upon the short, stockily built man with the little twinkling eyes, who stood only a few yards distant. Some instinct seemed to tell Arthur that this was the detective, that this was the one man he should avoid. As quick as thought, he turned on his heel and made a dash in the opposite direction. The detective noting the movement, started to follow him; but Herbert shouldering his way against some people who were standing between them, got in front of the detective and completely blocked his way.

"Move aside," said the officer angrily, "don't you see that that fellow is getting away? Move aside, I tell you!"

By this time the crowd in the corridor had become so dense that it was almost impassable. It was quite evident that Arthur had made his escape and in all probability was now out of harm's way. Herbert turned to the detective and said in a low tone:

"It's the wrong fellow, old man; it's all a mistake."

The little twinkling eyes looked searchingly into Herbert's face. What he saw there satisfied him. The pale face, the look of despair, the nervous manner were sufficient to indicate that the young man had just passed through a crisis. It would be useless to argue with him. The detective did not attempt it. He buttoned up his coat, pulled his hat down more firmly over his head, and walked away, muttering:

"Well, this is the queerest game I've ever been up against in all my career."

After the detective left him, Herbert moved over to one of the big windows in the post office corridor, and leaning his elbows on the sill, stood there for some time musing upon the incidents that had just occurred. He recalled with a feeling of sadness Tomlin's prophetic words: "An opportunity may come to you to do some big bit of work, and it will either break you or make you."

The opportunity had come much quicker than he had anticipated, and unless all signs failed it would prove to be the cause of his undoing. He wondered in a numb sort of way how he was ever going to face Blakeley. He had started out on this assignment with a great display of enthusiasm. Indeed, now that he looked back upon it he had acted with considerable presumption. He had as good as boasted of the ease with which he intended to handle the case, and now it was all ended in an inglorious fizzle. The thought of a face to face encounter with Blakeley was decidedly chilling. Blakeley, while possessing many charming personal traits, was one of the hardest taskmasters in the office. Herbert shrank at the thought of going before him without the coveted story. He even contemplated the notion of not returning to the office at all; but this bit of cowardice was soon overcome as a thought not to be seriously considered for an instant. He would return to the office; he would face the music like a man; and he would take his medicine—no matter how bitter—without making any faces.

He left the post office building to go to the Argus office; but somehow or other he could not summon up sufficient courage to undergo the dreadful ordeal; so he walked up Broadway, mingling with the crowd, looking in the shop windows and trying to forget the terrible details of the most unpleasant incident of his life. After awhile he turned off Broadway and walked in the direction of Fifth Avenue. When he had reached that fashionable thoroughfare he bent his footsteps towards Central Park. By this time it was late in the afternoon. The fashionable turnouts of the rich and the prosperous were going up the avenue, skilfully guided through the crowded street by richly liveried drivers who seemed to know every inch of the ground. Still Herbert walked on and on, seemingly unconscious of what he was doing. The approach of dusk brought him to his senses. He must go to the office and go there as quickly as possible.

He jumped on a 'bus that was going down-town, and at the intersection where the Avenue joins Broadway he alighted and boarded one of the surface cars. It was quite dusk when he reached the Argus office, and walking into the local room in an uncertain manner, he noticed that most of the men were out and that Blakeley was seated at his desk alone. The city editor was puffing at a big cigar, and did not notice the entrance of the young reporter.

Herbert was the first to speak.

"Mr. Blakeley," he said, in a hushed sort of voice.

The city editor turned around like a flash.

"Hello there, Harkins," he said eagerly; "I've been waiting for you all the afternoon. How did the thing pan out?"

"It didn't pan out at all," said Herbert in a hesitating, halting way.

"What do you mean?" cried the other, his tone perceptibly hardening.

"I mean that I have no story," this in a slightly firmer voice.

"No story?" shouted the other, "why what are you talking about anyhow? There must be a story."

"There was a story," rejoined Herbert, now throwing all precaution to the winds; "but I can't write it."

"Can't write it? Why, you're crazy, man. What are you talking about?"

The city editor was thoroughly angry now. He arose from his chair and stood towering before Herbert. In his rage he threw his freshly lighted cigar into the cuspidor with a savage movement of his hand. He stamped his foot on the floor fiercely.

"There is no use talking about this matter any longer. You go to your desk and write this thing and have your copy ready as soon as possible."

"I can't write it," said Herbert, now speaking in a voice that was scarcely audible.

Blakeley was silent, trying hard to control his rising passion. When he spoke his voice sounded almost like a hiss.

"You understand what this means, don't you—you know what it will cost you?"

"Yes," said Herbert, looking up; "I understand, and I resign my position as a reporter on the Argus."

"Your resignation is accepted," said the other shortly; "but I call upon you to do the work that you were assigned to perform, before leaving this office."

"I can't do it," said Herbert; "on my honor I cannot do it."

"But what explanation have you to give?"

Herbert looked up helplessly. For a moment a desire to tell the whole story to Blakeley took possession of him. The next minute it was dismissed as impracticable. Blakeley was a man without any heart or feeling. He felt convinced of this, and felt likewise that if the facts were once in the city editor's possession the story would have to be written regardless of the private anguish it might cause. So he stood there speechless before his superior.

"Go!" finally shouted Blakeley, pointing to the door. "But when you go remember that you go in disgrace. You are like an engineer who would leave his train in the middle of the journey, or a pilot who would desert his ship in a storm at sea. Go, and never let me see you again."

Herbert left the room with a flushed face and downcast eyes. He avoided the elevator. The thought of meeting with anyone at a time like this grated upon his feelings. He walked down the stairway with a heart as heavy as lead. He felt mortified and angry by turns. He mentally blamed Blakeley for his coarse manner and the ugly scolding he had given him. The next second he admitted to himself that Blakeley was fully justified in what he had said and done. Indeed, from the standpoint of the news and of duty, he could find no possible justification for his own conduct.

Presently he got out into Park Row and was soon in the midst of the pushing, bustling crowd. It was quite dark now, and the rush to the bridge was at its height. Myriads of electric lights shone brightly all about him. Cars rushed by, with motormen sounding their gongs continuously. Wagon drivers shouted and shrieked and pulled at their horses, and thousands of pedestrians laughed and shouted as they hurriedly went their way. Herbert, in a vague sort of way, wondered how they could all be so happy when he felt so miserable. Nothing seemed the same to him. Some mysterious change appeared to have overcome the face of New York since he had left his home early that morning; but in reality things moved on as before. Herbert's philosophy did not realize that the world moves on day by day and night by night, regardless of the joys or the woes of the individual.

He soon reached his lodgings and quietly let himself in the door by means of his latch-key. He struck a light and gazed about curiously at the familiar things in the little apartment. Everything in the room seemed to look at him in a reproachful manner. Strange as it may seem, it was some moments before he became accustomed to being alone. Then he picked up a book and tried to read; but it was a dismal failure. He walked the floor for a long, long while. There was a lump in his throat that he could not remove. Presently he sank down into a chair and dropped his bowed head into his hands on the table.

"I've lost my job," he groaned to himself. "I've done more than that. I've not only lost my place, but I've been retired in disgrace."

CHAPTER XVII
THE YOUNG REPORTER FINDS THAT THE DOOR OF OPPORTUNITY IS BARRED TO HIM

Herbert sat in the darkened room with his head bowed on the table for a very long while, thinking of the events that had taken place the previous twenty-four hours. First he was angry with himself for what he had done, and then felt humiliated at permitting Blakeley to abuse him in such a cruel manner; but with second thought came the conviction that even if he had it to go over again he would not have acted in a different manner. To have written the story even with Arthur at liberty would have meant lasting disgrace to Mary Black and her parents. He had paid a very dear price, but had averted that, which after all, was a very consoling thing. While he sat there Tomlin came into the room in his impetuous manner. He rushed over to Herbert and clapped him on the shoulders.

"Brace up, old man; don't sit here and mope as if you had lost your last friend in the world."

Herbert looked up at him and tried to smile; but the effort was a very sickly one.

Tomlin sat down beside his friend, and becoming serious, said:

"See here, old chap, I don't want to pry into your affairs, but why in the world did you throw Blakeley down in that cold-blooded fashion?"

"I didn't throw Blakeley down," began Herbert angrily.

But the other man held up his hand to stay the hot words, and replied in a low voice:

"But you did throw him down, and there is no possible way of proving anything to the contrary. Now you must have had a reason, and if you care to give it to me, I'll be glad to listen."

"I hope you won't consider me rude, or lacking in friendship," replied Herbert; "but really the circumstances make it impossible for me to tell you why I acted as I did."

"All right, old fellow," rejoined Tomlin, slapping Herbert on the back again; "I am satisfied whether you tell me or not. I believe in you and that is sufficient."

Shortly before noon the following day Herbert went to the office of the New York Sentinel and presented his card to the city editor. That individual sat in his roll-top chair and gazed at the bit of pasteboard musingly:

"So you want a job, do you? Well, I have heard of your name before, and I understand that you have done some creditable work. I might make a place for you here—"

"Could you?" inquired Herbert eagerly; "I'm sure if you would give me the chance I'd make good."

"I don't doubt it," said the city editor. Then as if the thought had just struck him: "By the way, how did you come to leave the Argus?"

Herbert flushed up at this, and the fact did not escape the attention of the keen-witted city editor of the Sentinel. He scrutinized his visitor with a steady eye. Herbert hesitated for some seconds, and then said slowly:

"Well, to tell the truth, that is a personal matter that I cannot explain."

"All right," said the other slowly, "that rests with you entirely."

"Can I have the position?" inquired Herbert.

"Well," said the other, rubbing his hand over his face and speaking slower than before, "I think you had better come in and see me again in the course of a day or so."

This was not very satisfactory, but Herbert had to make the best of it. He returned to his room for the purpose of writing some letters and later on took a walk. Two days after this incident he called at the Sentinel office, but found, to his disappointment, that the city editor was out of the city. Another day elapsed, and this time the man he was in search of was at his desk.

"Do you find that you will be able to employ me on the Sentinel?" asked Herbert.

"No," said the city editor decidedly; "no, I cannot find room for you."

"Is there any special reason for that decision?" asked Herbert with a sinking sensation in the region of the heart.

"Well," yawned the city editor, stretching his arms over his head, "I don't know that I should answer that question; but I will say that I had a talk with Blakeley, the city editor of the Argus, yesterday afternoon. You can draw your own conclusions."

Herbert did, and found that the conclusions were not very flattering to himself. In the course of the next two weeks he visited the local rooms of nearly every important newspaper in the city; but everywhere he met with the same experience. In short, he found himself blacklisted.

In the meantime he made every effort to preserve a cheerful demeanor. He wrote long letters home to his mother, but never mentioned the grave disaster which had overwhelmed him and which threatened to blight his future newspaper life. Fortunately he possessed a small sum of money which was on deposit in the saving fund. He had been prudent and thrifty from the time of his arrival in New York, and as a consequence was able to save small amounts of money in addition to the allowance which he sent to his mother with religious regularity. He drew this out now, and counting it over carefully found that, if necessary, it would be sufficient to pay his expenses for a month or so. But after all a month, and even two months pass very rapidly to a poor man who sees no immediate prospect of earning money. He noted with dismay that a whole week had been lost in his fruitless negotiations with the Sentinel, and that a longer period of time had passed by during the time he was applying to the other newspapers.

At this period he received a letter from Noah Brooks, saying that Mr. Anderson had told him of the big beat upon which he was working for the Argus, and wanting to know whether he had been able to carry it to a successful conclusion. The letter annoyed him, even coming from such an old and valued friend as the editor of the Cleverly Banner. However, he sent a courteous reply to his old friend, expressing regret at his failure to distinguish himself upon that particular piece of work.

Mr. Anderson, his former teacher, hearing that he had separated from the service of the Argus, called on him one evening.

"I am awfully sorry to hear this, Herbert, and I half suspect that it is the result of a quarrel with Blakeley."

"Yes," assented Herbert with a half smile, "there is no doubt about that. Blakeley quarreled all right. I think it was a one-sided quarrel; but there is no use in discussing it now."

"But there is use," insisted the other; "I'll go to see Blakeley at once and have this matter straightened out."

Herbert put a detaining hand on his arm, and said with great earnestness:

"Please don't do anything of the kind."

"But I will," cried the other.

"But you must not," corrected Herbert; "if you carry out your good intentions you will do me a great deal of harm. If you are really a friend of mine, I beg of you to stay away from the Argus office."

"But, my young man," said the teacher, "you are entirely too young to be so self opinionated. You should not have quarreled with Blakeley. It would have been much better if you had bent your will to his."

Herbert shook his head sadly. He was silent for a few moments, and then said with much gravity:

"You mean very well, but you cannot mend matters in this instance."

Mr. Anderson left the house looking very forlorn. He was anxious to help Herbert, and keenly felt his inability to do so.

Tomlin had been sent out on an assignment that took him to a remote part of the State. He remained away for a week, and Herbert was alone during all that period. Tomlin returned unexpectedly one evening, very anxious to hear the latest news regarding his friend and the papers. Herbert came in late that night. His white face, drooping mouth and hopeless eyes told their own story to Tomlin. However he tried to disguise the feeling that was within him, and said with assumed cheerfulness:

"Well, old boy, how have you made out in my absence? Have you tried any of the other papers?"

"Yes," said Herbert, "I have."

"Which one?"

"Everyone," said Herbert with a bitter smile, "at least everyone that is worth considering."

"Well, what are your prospects?"

"I have no prospects."

"No prospects—not even in the future?"

"No," retorted Herbert, the anger in his heart making him raise his voice to a high pitch; "not even in the future. To be plain with you, Tomlin, they all know about the circumstances under which I left the Argus, and they refuse to have anything to do with me. I am blacklisted. Do you understand that? I am blacklisted, and a disgraced man."

The tone of Herbert's voice no less than what he said shocked Tomlin very much; but he made no reply, and the two friends sat there for many minutes staring mutely at each other.

CHAPTER XVIII
WHEREIN A BLACK SHEEP SHOWS A DESIRE TO CHANGE HIS COLOR

One morning not long after the conversation which has been recorded in the previous chapter, Tomlin said to Herbert:

"See here, old chap, you are not going to throw up the sponge—I know you're not. You've got too much grit and pluck for any such thing as that."

"What do you mean?" asked Herbert, staring at him in an unmeaning way.

"What do I mean? I mean that you've got to employ strategy. When a soldier gets in a tight fix with the enemy, he uses the brains with which he is endowed for the purpose of extricating himself. So it is with the lawyer, with the business man and with mortals generally—"

"What in the world are you driving at?" interrupted Herbert.

"I know what I'm driving at," replied the other. "Listen to what I have to say, and then try to answer me intelligently. Can you write a good Sunday newspaper story?"

"Can I? Why you know—"

"Of course, of course I know," cut in Tomlin, "I only asked you that question as a matter of form. I want you to go out and get a first-class special story. Write it up in your most attractive style, typewrite it on the machine we have in this room, and give it to me by this time to-morrow."

The hearty manner of his friend furnished just the sort of inspiration that Herbert needed at that particular time. He went out during the day and visited the various places where he would be likely to obtain material for a special story. It grew quite late and he was still without anything upon which he could base the sort of article that would answer to the vivid description furnished by Tomlin. On his way back to his room he stopped at an Old Man's Home to enjoy a chat with the superintendent, who had been his friend while he was on the Argus, and had sometimes rendered him valuable assistance.

"Anything doing about here, Smith?" he asked.

"No," replied the superintendent, "not a thing. This is the slowest week we have had for a long while. It's as dull as dishwater."

"Sorry to hear that," responded Herbert; "I thought in a large community of this kind something was always happening."

"No," responded the other, "nothing worth printing. I've got a good joke on one of the old fellows upstairs, however. He was knocked out by a bat last night."

"By a bat?" queried Herbert.

"Yes. You see the old chap was a colonel in the Civil War—one of the bravest men that ever led a regiment. Well, while he was reading a bat flew into the room, and the things that happened during the next half hour were funny enough to make a sick cat well. The old colonel picked up his cane and chased that bird all around the room. The light bewildered the bat and caused it to flounder around so blindly that half of the ornaments in the room were broken. The colonel thought he had it at one time, though, and lifted up his cane to give the bird its death blow; but he missed by a hair, and instead of killing the pesky thing, he smashed two big vases that stood on the mantel-piece. Then when he made another lunge at it his stick went through an oil painting which I believe has been in his family for nearly a hundred years. It was daylight before that bird was thrust out of the room, and when the first streak of dawn penetrated into the apartment the floors and walls resembled some place which had just finished an unsuccessful siege with the enemy."

"Why, that's a pretty good story," cried Herbert quickly, "and if you will give me the privilege of talking to the old colonel and the chance to look at that room, I will thank you to the day of my death."

The superintendent was only too well pleased to do this. Herbert obtained a picture of the valiant soldier, and borrowing a camera from one of the inmates, made a photograph of the dismantled room. He hurried home, and before midnight had succeeded in grinding out an exceedingly interesting special which was entitled "The Story of the Union Soldier and the Bat." He turned this over to Tomlin in the morning, and when they met in the evening again that young man said with a considerable degree of self-satisfaction:

"Your story is accepted and will be printed, and you will be paid for it on the first of the month."

"But I—they—" began Herbert.

"Oh," interrupted the other impatiently, "I know what you are going to say. I know that you are blacklisted, but that has nothing to do with the case. A man must earn a living, and you have a right to your bread and butter. Besides this is a justifiable deception. I am going to keep on selling your stuff as my own as long as you have wit enough to write. The articles will be typewritten, and the editors who buy them from me will not know the difference except," with a little laugh, "they will be a little more brilliant than the kind I am in the habit of writing."

"You think it's all right?" ventured Herbert.

"Of course it's all right. Where's the harm? No name is signed to the articles. The newspapers get the worth of their money. The readers are satisfied. You are reimbursed, and I am gratified. What more would you want?"

Herbert soon came around to this way of thinking, and then and there started in on another article, which proved equally as saleable as the first. Elated by the success of these two articles, he planned a series of Sunday specials, chiefly sketches of odd phases of life in New York City. He was industry personified, and worked so adroitly in gathering his facts that his identity was fully concealed. One morning, just as he was about to leave the house he received a letter; and on tearing open the envelope, found that it was dated from a small town in the northern part of Connecticut. It was as follows:

"DEAR HERBERT:

"I would be an ingrate of the meanest type if I did not write to you and acknowledge the great debt which I owe to you now, and which I will continue to owe till the day of my death. I fully realize that if it had not been for your interference and kindness I would have been arrested, and myself and the members of my family disgraced. But sometimes bad beginnings have good results, and the merest incidents prove to be the turning point in a man's career. I am satisfied now that the little episode which occurred at the post office a few weeks ago is going to prove the making of me. I know that I have been indolent and worthless; that I was foolish enough to contract bad and vicious associations, and that I have been guilty of many disreputable things. Somehow or other I went along doing these things without thinking of the meanness that was involved in them. Looking back upon them now, I can see very readily how little incidents repeated many times led to bad habits, and how these bad habits were gradually undermining my whole character.

"I do not ask you to believe me, but I am going to tell you just the same, that from the instant you gave me the kindly warning in the post office building I made up my mind that if I were given the opportunity I would lead a better life in the future. I am now making this effort with all the courage at my command. It's a hard job, but I believe that I am going to come out a winner. I have secured honest employment in this little town, and I intend to remain here till I am fully satisfied that I am fit to associate with manly and self-respecting persons like yourself. Kindly consider this letter sent in confidence, and not to be revealed till you hear from me further.

"Very truly yours,
"ARTHUR BLACK."

Herbert was delighted with this missive. It repaid him for the great sacrifice he had made—not for Arthur Black—but for his sister. His first thought was to call on Mary and assure her that her brother was alive and well; but upon mature reflection he abandoned this as being unwise. From that day, however, Herbert put more heart into his work. He still depended upon his voluntary contributions to the newspapers, and while he longed for a permanent position on the staff of one of the large dailies, he felt that he would have to bide his time before he reached such a desirable post.

During these days he often thought of his father, and more than once he recalled the dramatic scene when his father and the strange visitor were seated at the table together in their little home at Cleverly. He had frequently resolved to run out the mystery of that night, and now he vowed it with more than usual vehemence. Everywhere he went he tried to discover some signs of the queer stranger. It seemed a hopeless task, but he resolved to persist in it till the end. One evening, while he was walking down Cortlandt street, his gaze was attracted by a big, broad-shouldered man who was walking along the street four or five yards in advance of him. There was something very familiar about those bulky shoulders. He looked again, and as his glance traveled upward he suddenly realized that the man had a shock of bushy red hair. Recognition was instantaneous; it was the man he had been looking for for so long. He pushed his way through the crowd, and at one time was almost able to reach the mysterious person by stretching out his hands; but at that critical moment a heavily laden truck intervened, and the queer one gained several yards on him. It was evident that he was making for the ferry house to take the boat which ran to Jersey City. Just before they reached the pier the bell began to ring its warning signal. The crowd hurried. The man with the red hair and the bulky shoulders ran rapidly towards the boat, with Herbert after him panting for breath.

"Hurry up!" shouted the gateman to the approaching crowd.

The big man redoubled his speed, and just as he entered the ferry slip and got aboard the bell rang for the second time, the iron gate was slammed to with a bang, and Herbert found himself standing on the wharf, gazing at the boat churning its way towards the shores of New Jersey.

CHAPTER XIX
PERSISTENCE HAS ITS REWARD AND HERBERT FINALLY MEETS THE MYSTERIOUS STRANGER

Herbert Harkins was now consumed with a burning desire to meet the mysterious stranger. He had an actual interest in clearing the memory of his father; but above and beyond that he was now filled with a boyish curiosity which insisted upon being satisfied. The thought of the stranger occupied his waking hours, and even disturbed his rest at night. When he was out of doors he stared at all the big men he happened to meet, in order to discover, if possible, a burly man with broad shoulders and a shock of red hair. At times this peculiar quest seemed so absurd that he felt like abandoning it altogether; but such periods of depression were invariably followed by a resolution to persevere till he had accomplished his desire.

This sort of thing went on day after day without bringing any practical results. Just when Herbert was beginning to tire of it, the thought flashed across his mind that publicity was frequently a way of obtaining things that could not be found by ordinary efforts. In other words, he flew to the personal columns of the daily newspapers for assistance. The result of this was the following advertisement which appeared one morning in the New York Herald:

"Will the stranger who called on David Harkins at Cleverly very late one night about five years ago kindly send his address to H. H., care of General Delivery, Post Office. By doing so he may be the instrument of redeeming the memory of a good man."

Herbert was very much pleased with the phrasing of this advertisement. There was an air of romance about it that appealed quite strongly to his youthful fancy. The day after its appearance he hurried to the post office with the expectation of receiving a letter, but he was doomed to disappointment. No reply of any kind had been received. On the second day he called at the post office again, and this time was rewarded by the receipt of a very much soiled postal card. The writer informed him that he had called on David Harkins at Cleverly about five years ago and would be glad to meet the person who was in quest of information. The address given was that of a low-grade lodging house on the Bowery. Herbert felt a trifle disappointed at the tone of this communication, but nevertheless resolved to run it out to the end. He visited the Bowery that afternoon, and was received by a short, stout man with a very red nose and a somewhat husky voice.

"You sent me this postal card," said Herbert, exhibiting the square piece of manila board.

"Yes," said the other, with a leer, "what is there in it for me if I give you the information you are after?"

"I don't know that that has anything to do with it," said Herbert.

"Oh, yes," retorted the other, with a chuckle, "it has everything to do with it, my young chappie. I'm a business man."

"A business man?" queried Herbert.

"Yes, sir, a business man. My motto is, no cash no information. That's plain enough, isn't it?"

"Too plain," said Herbert, picking up his hat and starting towards the door.

"Hold on!" cried the other, jumping up; "I don't want much from you, and I'll tell you anything you wish to know."

"I have no doubt of it," replied Herbert; "but unfortunately you are not the man I want."

"Oh, yes, I am," insisted the other eagerly, "I'm the man that called on David Harkins at Cleverly."

Herbert shook his head and shrugged his shoulders; then as if it were an afterthought, he turned to the seedy-looking person and said:

"Do you insist that you are the identical man who called on David Harkins?"

"I insist," repeated the man, trying to draw himself up in a dignified way.

"Now, I am sure that I have no business with you," said Herbert, "because it so happens that the man who called on David Harkins had bright red hair—it was bushy, too, while you are almost bald-headed and your hair is black."

The fellow snickered a little at this, and said:

"I lost me hair durin' a very bad attack o' fever."

Herbert could not forbear smiling himself.

"I suppose the color turned, too, at the same time."

"Yes," answered the man, "it did indeed. You needn't laugh. Scientific men will tell you that a man's hair often changes color in a single night."

"Well, good-by," said Herbert, "I'll leave you to settle that with the scientists."

Three weeks passed by after this amusing episode and Herbert received no further replies from the personal that he had inserted in the Herald. He was reading the paper one afternoon, and while running his trained eye down the many columns of small advertisements, happened to see his own name in print. He looked closer, and this is what he read:

"If Herbert Harkins, son of the late David Harkins, of Cleverly, New Jersey, will make his whereabouts known to the undersigned, he may learn of something to his advantage. Write without delay to Captain Thomas Janson, Anchor Inn, Jersey City, N. J."

Feverish with anxiety, Herbert immediately sent a letter in response to this advertisement. Within forty-eight hours after that he received an answer, written in a large, sprawling hand, inviting him to call on Captain Janson at his domicile in Jersey City. He responded without delay. He found Anchor Inn to be an obscure hotel in a deserted part of the town. It was a popular resort for seafaring men. Upon inquiry for Captain Janson, he was informed that the Captain had removed that very morning to a new two-story house which he had erected on the outskirts of the city. He had left a message for Herbert, however, giving him explicit directions where he could find his new domicile.

Herbert listened very carefully, and then made his way to the address that had been given him. He found it to be the quaintest looking house it had ever been his good fortune to gaze upon. The front of it was shaped like the prow of a boat, and under the eaves of the house was a wooden effigy of a mermaid, shaped and painted like those used upon sailing craft in the Eastern waters. He rang the bell, and the call was answered by a colored youth dressed up in blue clothing, with brass buttons, to represent a cabin boy. He was ushered into a small, low-ceilinged apartment which resembled the captain's quarters upon a boat. The beds on either side of the room were fitted up to resemble bunks. The windows had been so constructed that they were perfect reproductions of port holes. A little desk, a brass-rimmed clock, such as can be seen in the cabins of pleasure yachts, a coil of rope, a large marine glass, and cheap colored pictures of the admirals of the United States Navy adorned the walls of this strangely furnished room.

Presently the door of an adjoining apartment opened and a big, brawny man, with the rolling gait of a sailor, entered the room. His face was as red as a boiled lobster; his hands were thick-skinned and broad. He had wide shoulders and—this detail made an immediate impression upon Herbert—he also possessed a heavy shock of red hair. The identification was complete. This man, beyond a doubt, was the person who had been with his father on that eventful night.

"Avast there, my hearty!" shouted the newcomer, putting out his broad hand to meet the outstretched palm of his caller; "what are you doing aboard my craft?"

"My name is Herbert Harkins," said the young man, "and I came here in response to your letter."

The seaman stopped short with an exclamation on the tip of his tongue. He stood in the center of the room with his hands on his hips and rolled his head from side to side as he stared at Herbert with unblinking eyes. The scrutiny appeared to satisfy him.

"So you're Dave Harkins' boy, are you? Well, you look like him; you look like him just as he appeared when he was a young man. You're different from him in some ways, but the resemblance is there just the same. You're more like a chip off the old block than the old block itself. Now, boy, take a seat on that steamer chair there, get out your log book and tell me all about your journey through life."

"All right, sir," replied Herbert, taking the proffered seat; "I'll do so."

"By the way," interrupted the Captain, "before you talk about yourself, tell me about your father."

"You know that father is dead?" began Herbert.

"Yes, I know that," answered the other, "but I want some details about it."

"All right, I'll try to give them to you."

"By the way," he interrupted again, as Herbert started to talk, "will you have a glass of grog to wet your whistle?"

"No, sir," replied Herbert, "I don't drink."

"Good for you; you're a good deal better without it; but an old salt like myself couldn't do without his pipe and his grog, especially in his old days."

Herbert then proceeded to tell the old sailor all about his father, and when he spoke of the mysterious midnight visit and the cloud of false rumors that had arisen therefrom the Captain's face clouded and he walked up and down the floor of his little cabin shaking his fist.

"The lubbers!" he shouted, "they ought to have been tied to the mast and given a dose of a cat o' nine tails."

Having finished this part of his narrative, Herbert then proceeded to tell the story of his own life, and at its conclusion the old salt put out his brawny hand, and taking Herbert's, gave it a hearty grasp.

"Your story is mighty interesting. I'm mighty glad to hear it, and I think I am in a position to be your friend."

"I am glad of that," responded Herbert, "and I'm very curious to find out the real meaning of that midnight visit."

"I'll give it to you, my boy, and in mighty quick order. I was a boyhood chum of your father. We grew up together, went to school together, and one never had a thing that wasn't shared by the other. I had no idea of the sea in my youth; but shortly after I got to be a boy of about your age I was entrusted with a sum of money belonging to another person. I was a sort of trustee. In an evil moment some fellow came along and showed me how it would be possible to double the money without any risk. I tried it, and lost every cent. While I was in this condition, I was called upon to make an accounting of the trust money. In my extremity I went to your father and explained everything. He gave me every penny that he had in the world in order to make good the loss, and my reputation was saved and I had learned a lesson that I have never forgotten since then. I was a wild boy in my younger days. I owed a great deal of money, and finally determined to take to the sea as a means of cooling down my hot blood. During the next ten years I sailed over every part of the civilized globe. I became a master and traded extensively in the Chinese seas. I was fortunate, made money, and finally came home to retire upon my savings.

"The first man I thought of," said the Captain, leaning back in his easy chair, "was Dave Harkins. I determined to hunt him up and pay him the few hundred dollars he had so generously given me at a critical time in my life. I got to Cleverly late at night; the hotel was closed so that I was unable to secure accommodations there. The thought struck me that I might find Harkins at home. I went to his house, and fortunately found him at a moment when he needed my help just as I had formerly needed his. I compelled him to take that thousand dollars, and I made a condition that he was not to tell of my whereabouts until I got ready to make myself known to the world. I wanted to clear up all of my old debts and to rehabilitate myself before my old friends before I revealed my identity. After leaving him I went to New York, and carrying out a program that had already been arranged, went abroad to settle up some business interests that I had in Liverpool. I came back, only to hear that David Harkins was dead. I was told that the family had moved from Cleverly, and accepted the report without attempting to verify it. Years went by, but I was never quite satisfied. I hunted around in a vague sort of way to find Harkins' boy. Only last week it occurred to me that a personal in the Herald might bring some results, and thank goodness it did, because here you are with me in the flesh."

"I am very grateful to hear all of this," said Herbert after the old sailor had finished; "I can assure you that it makes me very happy indeed. I never doubted my father at any time; but it is a great satisfaction to have the whole matter settled and to have these painful rumors dispelled as you have dispelled them."

The Captain arose from his chair, took a turn or two around the room, and then putting his arm around Herbert's shoulder, said:

"My boy, we'll dispel them in such a way that they'll never be heard of again. Mark one thing down, and mark it down plain: I'm your friend, and your friend for life."

CHAPTER XX
IN WHICH A STAIN IS REMOVED FROM THE MEMORY OF AN INNOCENT MAN

Herbert remained with Captain Janson for several hours. The man and the boy were mutually attracted. After some further conversation regarding David Harkins, the sailor said:

"Now tell me your story."

Herbert did so as briefly and as modestly as possible. He told of his difficulty with the Argus; but discreetly avoided all reference to Arthur Black and the manner in which he had saved him at the expense of his own position.

"My boy," said the Captain, when he had concluded, "it's all right; don't worry about these little things. The first thing we have to do is to straighten out the memory of your father with the people of Cleverly. You know how these stories stick in small communities. My boy, we'll hoist sail and bear down on the port of Cleverly at once, and when we land there we'll let the natives know a thing or two. We'll let 'em know that David Harkins was one of Nature's noblemen, and now that he's gone to Davy Jones' locker, he has left a friend and a son who will take care of his memory."

The following day they both took the train and went to Cleverly. Their first visit was to the office of the Cleverly Banner, where Captain Jansen was introduced to Noah Brooks. The editor and the sailor had not talked for ten minutes before they became fast friends. Presently they were joined by Horace Coke, the lawyer, who had always been a friend of the Harkins family, and who was delighted with the turn things had taken. After a general conversation in which all hands joined, the sailor suddenly pounded his hand on the desk, and said earnestly:

"Messmates, I'm here for a purpose, and a specific purpose. Dave Harkins was an honest man. I want everybody else to know that fact. How can I do it?"

Noah Brooks scratched his head for awhile, and then said musingly:

"You might print a story in the Banner, telling all about your visit that night, and explaining how you came to give him those ten $100 bills. How does that strike you?"

"Pardon me," interrupted the lawyer, "but that doesn't strike me very favorably. It would look forced. Besides everybody knows that Brooks is a friend of Herbert Harkins, and some people might be inclined to think the story was a little overdrawn."

"Yes, that's so," admitted Brooks, "but I hardly know how you can get around it in any other way. Besides, I would do this thing freely and voluntarily. It is not a question of expense or money."

"Money!" shouted the old sailor, "who said anything about money? I want you to understand that money is not to stand in the way of this business. There isn't any expenditure that I could make that would help the memory of Dave Harkins that I wouldn't undertake."

"Do you mean that?" asked Brooks.

"Of course I mean it. By the way, while I am here I would like to do something for this town of yours. What do you need just now?"

The lawyer laughed at this.

"You talk like a millionaire."

"Well," responded the sailor, "I am not a millionaire, but I've got enough to live on and a little over, too, and if I can make somebody else feel happy I'm going to do it."

"You asked me just now," said the lawyer musingly, "what you could do for the town."

"Yes, I did."

"Well," responded the other, "a little fountain in the middle of the main street wouldn't be a bad thing. It would be the means of slaking the thirst of both man and beast. We had one there some years ago, and it was mighty useful; but it's worn out now, and we have no means of replacing it."

"What will it cost?" asked the sailor.

"Not more than two thousand dollars," responded Mr. Coke; "that would finish the whole thing in first-class style."

"It's a go!" shouted the sailor, jumping up; "get the thing up in good shape, and get it up as quickly as possible."

Then and there specifications were drawn up, advertisements given out and the draft of a communication made to city councils. Within thirty days the whole thing had been completed and was ready for dedication. On the morning fixed for the celebration it slowly dawned on Herbert's mind that the sailor and the lawyer had a fixed purpose in all that they had done, and this purpose was only now beginning to unfold itself. He got his first inkling of this when he noticed the little silver plate on the side of the fountain, saying that it been erected by Captain Thomas Janson to the memory of his lifelong friend, David Harkins.

Mrs. Harkins wept a great deal when she saw this plate, which was a very good thing for her, because it relieved her pent up feelings and enabled her to recall memories of the dead without doing her any serious injury. Herbert, on the other hand, was flushed with conscious pride. A committee of the city councils had the affair in charge, and they made Mrs. Harkins, Herbert and Captain Janson the guests of honor. The Mayor of the city made the speech accepting the fountain, and then Captain Janson, as the closest friend of David Harkins, was called on for a few remarks.

The speech that he made that day was one of the most remarkable that had ever been delivered in the town. It told the story of the life of David Harkins, and how he had once befriended the speaker during what he firmly believed was the crisis of his life. He then related in great detail how he had come to Cleverly late that night and forced his old friend to accept the ten $100 bills. Thus, without making any direct reference to the ancient rumors that had flourished in the town, the stain attached to the memory of David Harkins was removed in the most effective manner possible. John Black and his daughter were present at the ceremonies, and at the conclusion of the set speeches Mr. Black arose and paid a fervent tribute to the integrity of David Harkins. Altogether everything was done in the most complete manner, and the affair was a great success and a red letter day in the history of Cleverly.

The story of the event was told in a full page report in the current issue of the Banner. To the delight of Mr. Brooks, Herbert had volunteered to write the report, and it proved to be one of the best pieces of reporting that had ever been done for the local paper. Captain Janson was the hero of the occasion. He remained in Cleverly for about a week, and he spent his money so lavishly and with such utter unconcern that he came to be looked upon as a modern Monte Cristo.

During his stay he formed quite an intimacy with Noah Brooks, and it was not very long before the whole-hearted sailor and the eccentric editor were almost indispensable to each other. Sitting in the Banner office one day Janson said:

"See here, Brooks, Cleverly looks to me like a good port in a storm. It strikes me that it would be a pretty good place for an old worn out hulk like Captain Janson. I've got a great notion to gather my stores and anchor here for the rest of my life."

Brooks thought so, too, and said he felt satisfied that the Captain would never have cause to regret making the change in his dwelling place. The sight of the two old men sitting on the porch exchanging stories of the varied experiences they had undergone during their stormy lives was a picture not to be forgotten very quickly. At least Herbert Harkins thought so, and when he finally took the train for his return to New York the pretty little scene remained engraved upon his memory.

CHAPTER XXI
IN WHICH A TELEPHONE CALL PRODUCES SOME UNEXPECTED RESULTS

Herbert returned to New York from Cleverly in the gayest of spirits. He was happier than he had been for years, and was filled with a desire to communicate this light-hearted feeling to everyone that he met. The fact that the long standing cloud had been removed from the memory of his father made him forget his own troubles for the time at least. A week before everything had appeared dark and gloomy; but now the dawn had arrived and the earth assumed a cheerful appearance. With the light-heartedness of youth, he looked forward to a future of prosperity and uninterrupted happiness.

The time was within a month of Christmas, and before leaving Cleverly he had exacted a promise from his mother that she would come to New York on the eve of the festival and stay with him over the holidays. He was already mentally planning out the treat that would be given her on her arrival in the metropolis. It was in this mood that he hurried to his apartments. He found Tomlin at home, and opening and closing the door boisterously, shouted:

"Hello Tomlin, old fellow! I want you to jump up and shake hands with a very happy man."

Tomlin did jump up and did shake hands with his friend; but he said nothing, gazing on the other with an expectant air. Receiving no response to his silent inquiry, he asked:

"Have you fallen heir to a fortune?"

"No," said Herbert, "something better than that."

"Have you obtained a permanent position on one of the big papers?"

"No," replied Herbert, and this time a little sadly, "not that."

"Well, what in the world is it?" asked the other.

"Simply this," replied Herbert, speaking hurriedly and with some feeling; "after a number of anxious years I have succeeded in clearing the memory of my father from a stain that has rested upon it ever since his death."

Very rapidly he sketched the events that had followed one another from the time he had read the little personal in the Herald until the unveiling of the memorial fountain in Cleverly.

Tomlin whistled.

"This is news indeed, and I never knew a thing about it. Why didn't you tell me?"

"I owe you an apology for that," said Herbert contritely, "but I was a victim of circumstances. After my interview with the old sea captain I missed you, and found it necessary to go to Cleverly immediately. Besides that I had a strong desire to complete the whole business so that I might give you the story in full when we met."

"Don't mention it," said the other heartily, his eyes glistening with the pleasure he felt. "Why the thing has the flavor of a romance from real life. Say, it would make a bully story for the Argus."

Herbert raised his hand in protest.

"Don't think of such a thing, Tomlin!" he exclaimed. "I am not desirous of any publicity just at this time. I wouldn't have Blakeley even hear my name or to see it, at least not for some time to come. I know that he feels very bitterly towards me, and I realize that he has a real justification for that feeling. Some day I may be able to win back his good opinion."

"I hope so," fervently ejaculated Tomlin; then as if the thought had just struck him: "Why not make the attempt now?"

"It is not possible now," said Herbert in a positive tone, which conveyed a distinct desire to close the subject.

"By the way," said Tomlin, "you will have to get down to work. You've been wasting a lot of your time when you should have been toiling for your bread and butter. I've got an order here for three specials, and you will have to turn them out before the end of the week."

"I'm your man," responded Herbert enthusiastically. Then looking at his friend fondly, he added:

"Say, Tomlin, how can I ever repay you for your goodness to me?"

"By never speaking about it," was the crisp reply.

Herbert started in immediately and began working on the specials that had been ordered for the following week. He had to go out for several days and nights in succession in order to obtain the material, but once that was in hand he worked quickly and industriously. One of the articles was a graphic description of the entrance to the Brooklyn bridge at the rush hour in the evening. The subject was not new by any means; but Herbert handled it with such cleverness and originality that it made a very readable page in the Sunday issue of one of the enterprising newspapers. Another of the specials was a description of Chinatown at night, couched in such phraseology as to make the reader believe that the scenes so graphically described were taking place in the heart of one of the cities of old China instead of actually being enacted in the midst of the American metropolis. The third article gave the impressions of a man who went to the very top of one of the highest buildings on Manhattan Island and viewed the surrounding country.

The Argus office was only a few blocks from the lodgings of the two young men. While Herbert was hard at work one night, Tomlin rushed in unexpectedly, and said in agitated tones:

"I've got a sensational tip that I want you to run out for me. I am tied up on another story now, and there is no one in the office. It may be nothing, or it may be a good thing; but if you are willing to tackle it I will guarantee that you will not lose anything by the operation."

"Don't talk about losses," said Herbert impatiently; "tell me what you want."

"Well," said the other; "I was around at the precinct police station a little while ago. The telephone bell rang while I was in the room. The house sergeant was sound asleep, snoring like a log, so I took the liberty of responding to the call. When I got my ear to the receiver a very feminine voice said:

"'Is this the police station?'

"'Yes ma'am,' I replied, wondering what was coming next.

"'Well,' said the sweet voice again, 'a burglar has broken into our house and I have him locked in the sitting room, and I will be very much obliged indeed if you will send an officer here at once to take the man into custody.'

"Just in the most matter of fact manner imaginable," cried Tomlin. "Could anything be more picturesque or interesting? Here is a woman who is not afraid of a burglar. She calmly telephones for the police to come and arrest him. I think that's a peach of a story, and if you have any red blood in your veins you will grab your hat and coat and start off on the story before I am able to say ten more words."

This was precisely what Herbert did. In less than a minute's time he was at the door, and turning to Tomlin, said:

"Where's the house? What was the number?"

"The cabby knows all about it," said Tomlin, pointing to a stout man who was sitting on the high seat of a cab in front of the door.

"What's that?" asked Herbert.

"That's the cabby," replied Tomlin; "you don't suppose I would come here without furnishing you with all the conveniences necessary to do the job. There's a policeman in plain clothes on the inside of the cab. All you have to do is to go with him, help him to make the arrest, and then write up the story. I'll call here again in an hour and get the copy. If it proves to be a beat, I'll give it to Blakeley in the morning and quietly let him know that you have sent it in as a partial act of retribution for the scurvy manner in which you treated him on that other big scoop."

"Tomlin, I wish you would stop talking about that," said Herbert impatiently; "but I'll do the best I can with this story." And with a farewell shout he jumped into the cab, pulled the door to with a slam and was whirled in the direction of upper New York. The cab driver had evidently been given an extra fee for speed, because he lashed his horse unmercifully, and the vehicle went whirling up Broadway at a gait which terrified chance pedestrians and aroused the ire of sleepy policemen. Once the hub of the wheel struck another team that was coming down-town, and for several seconds Herbert felt that their team was about to be wrecked; but by some lucky chance the wheels became extricated and the cab once more resumed its upward and onward journey. Finally, after many minutes had passed, it turned off the main highway into a side street. Herbert noticed by glancing at a lamp on the side of the thoroughfare that they had turned into West 69th street. Presently the cab stopped, and when Herbert and the officer had alighted, the cabby, pointing towards a brownstone house with the tip of his whip, said:

"That's your house, boys."

Herbert looked up at the dwelling, and something familiar about it arrested his attention. He looked again to make sure, but there could be no doubt about it.

It was the home of John Black. Herbert stood on the sidewalk for some seconds, half dazed at this entirely unexpected discovery. He wondered curiously what fatality it was that had brought him to this house on such a strange errand at such an hour of the night; but presently he aroused himself. Speculation was in vain; action was necessary. After a few whispered instructions to the officer, he walked up the high steps and rang the bell.

CHAPTER XXII
PROVING THAT BAD PERSONS, LIKE BAD PENNIES, ARE CONSTANTLY REAPPEARING

After ringing the bell of the house, Herbert waited for a long time, but there was no response. Instantly his whole being was thrown into a fever of impatience and unrest. He imagined all sorts of terrible things. His mind was filled with terror. What if he had arrived on the scene too late? What if some crime had been committed in the dead of the night? Curiously enough, during that mental review he never thought of John Black or his wife. The one person constantly in his mind was Mary Black.

He rang the bell a second time. This time it was done fiercely, angrily. He listened eagerly, but received no immediate response, and then consulted with the policeman upon the advisability of going to the rear of the house and breaking in. While they were talking a sound was heard at the parlor window, and the next moment it was thrown open. A head was pushed cautiously out of the window. Herbert recognized it at a glance. It was Mary Black. He was on the top step now, and leaning over, said quietly so as not to alarm the girl:

"Mary."

She started at the sound of a familiar voice, and peering out into the gloom, exclaimed in genuine surprise:

"Herbert Harkins!"

"Yes, Mary," he answered; "what is the difficulty?"

"Oh, I'm terribly frightened," she cried, "someone has broken into the house. I don't know who it is, except that it is a man. I was reading in my room when I heard a grating sound at the kitchen door. Presently it was opened, and footsteps could be heard going into the dining room. Then all was silent for awhile. I came down the front stairway about half way, and leaning over the banister, looked in the dining room. The fellow's back was to me. He was seated at the table calmly eating some cold meat that he had taken out of the refrigerator. He had a couple of bottles of papa's wine, also, and was drinking that with great relish. Scarcely knowing what to do, I crept back to my room. Both papa and mamma had gone out for the evening, and I had no idea when they would return home. While I was in my room, in an agony of fear, I heard the fellow come upstairs. He went back into the library, and securing a large tablecloth, filled it with the silverware and other valuable things that he had carried from the dining room. Then he sank back into a large arm chair and calmly went to sleep. It was then that I conceived the idea of sounding the alarm. I pulled the doors of the library to and locking them securely, came down to the hall, where we have a telephone, and notified the police."

"Good!" exclaimed Herbert at the conclusion of this narrative, "you have acted very discreetly. Is the fellow still asleep?"

"No," she replied; "he evidently awakened a few minutes ago, because I hear him in the room. He has discovered the fact that he is a prisoner, and I am sure will either jump through one of the back windows or break open the door."

Herbert immediately sent the policeman to the rear of the house, with instructions to arrest anybody who might attempt to escape from that part of the property. Another patrolman fortunately passing by at this time, volunteered to guard the front of the house, while Herbert went in to grapple with the intruder.

Mary was quite solicitous for Herbert's safety, as was only natural.

"Please be careful," she said; "he may be a dangerous character. Don't you think you had better send one of the officers up?"

"No," said Herbert, "I think I'll tackle this job myself."

He felt some apprehension, but being a man, did not propose to display it before a girl for whom he had so much regard as Mary Black.

He crept up the stairs silently, armed with a pistol which Tomlin had thoughtfully provided. He heard a great knocking on the doors of the library, and going there immediately, turned the key and threw them open. The man within, surprised at this bold movement, retreated to the rear of the room. There was no light, but Herbert could see his figure dimly moving in the gloom.

"Surrender or you will be shot!" he shouted sternly.

For answer the burglar drew a pistol from his pocket, and aiming at Herbert, pulled the trigger. There was a flash of light and then all was silence. Herbert felt a tickling sensation like a pin prick on the back of his right hand. He lifted it, and noticed that the bullet had just grazed the top of his hand, which was already bleeding. Smarting with anger, he raised his own pistol and fired. It went far of the mark, but it produced results, for a heavy bass voice coming out of the darkness shouted:

"Stop shooting, and I'll surrender."

Herbert put his pistol away, and striking a match, lit the gas. The burglar was crouching in a corner of the room back of a book-case. His clothing seemed to be in tatters. Herbert strode over to where he was and grabbing him by the arm, pulled him out. The man turned round with a whine:

"You're not going to hurt me, are you?" he said.

Something in the voice attracted Herbert at once. He scrutinized the bleared face and recognized in it the countenance of Harry Adler. The discovery aroused his indignation.

"You scoundrel!" he shouted, raising his voice in his anger. "What do you mean by coming here and trying to rob these people. Aren't you satisfied with the injury you have already done to this family? You have taken their boy away from them, and now to cap the climax, you are low enough and despicable enough to come and try to rob them of their property."

"What family?" asked Adler, looking up at the young man with a sullen gaze.

"What family?" ejaculated Herbert, "do you mean to say that you did not know that this was John Black's house?"

"No," was the reply with an ugly leer. "I didn't know it was John Black's house. I was hard up; I had to get something; I needed money. This looked like an easy thing. How could I tell whose crib I was trying to crack?"

"Well," said Herbert bitterly, "you put your head in the noose this time all right You've been caught red-handed, and you'll go to jail without doubt."

"How do you know this?" asked Adler, with sudden defiance.

"Because the house is guarded back and front," was the reply; "because I have caught you in the act and you are my prisoner now, and I don't propose to permit you to escape."

The burglar looked at his antagonist in a blank sort of way for a moment, then a glitter of intelligence and cunning suddenly illumined the fishy eyes and the sodden face.

"If you permit the police to take me up to-night you'll regret it to the very end of your life."

Something in the man's manner and in the tone of his voice arrested Herbert's attention. Some instinctive feeling seemed to tell him that these words were not mere bravado. He turned to the culprit:

"Why? Why do you say this?"

"Because," exclaimed Adler, in a shrill voice, "if you have me arrested I'll squeal. I'll tell the truth and the whole truth about young Arthur Black. He came to New York with me as my partner. He was concerned in that dirty get-rich-quick business. I'll turn State's evidence, and if I go to jail he'll go with me, and you can bet your sweet life that the Black family will be mighty unhappy before I get through with them."

Herbert was the picture of distress. The man watched him with a leer. With all his defects, Adler possessed acute intelligence and he realized that Herbert was more deeply interested in Mary Black than he was willing to acknowledge. Knowing this, he felt that he had struck his captor in his weakest spot. It did not take Herbert long to decide. Turning to the unfortunate man, he said:

"Suppose you are released, what then?"

"Then mum's the word," replied the burglar, "I'll not squeal; I'll go about my business and let you and your friends go about yours."

"Wait a minute," was Herbert's comment. Going to the foot of the stairs, he called for Mary Black. She came up very much agitated. She peeped in at the burglar, who still lay in a heap on the floor, and shuddered at the sight. Herbert whispered to her.

"Mary, this man deserves to be arrested and imprisoned; but I have a great notion to let him go. He is an old Cleverly boy. It's Harry Adler. He never did amount to much, but it might be an act of charity to permit him to go in peace this time."

Her eyes brightened and the color returned to her face. In her enthusiasm she took Herbert by both hands, exclaiming:

"I agree with you thoroughly, and I think you're simply great to act so generously with a man who is at your mercy."

While this conversation was going on the policemen who had been patiently waiting in the front and rear of the house, tiring of their long watch, came inside and walked up the stairway. As they joined the group, Herbert turned to the man who had accompanied him, and said:

"Gentlemen, this is all a deplorable error. This gentleman is a distant relative of the family. In the confusion he was taken for an intruder. The family is very much mortified, and hopes that nothing more will be said about the matter."

The policemen smiled at this and bowing their heads in acquiescence left the house, chuckling in audible tones. Such scenes were not unfamiliar to the members of the metropolitan police force. As soon as they had gotten out of sight, Herbert turned to Adler, and in a tone freighted with anger and contempt, exclaimed:

"Go!"

The man looked up out of the corner of his eye as if to assure himself that there was no treachery intended, and then slunk downstairs and out into the street.

As he withdrew Mary turned to Herbert and then suddenly gave a terrible scream.

"Why, what's the matter, Mary?" he cried anxiously, rushing over to her.

"Oh that, that!" she exclaimed, pointing to his right hand, which was now almost covered with blood; "you have been shot. You are wounded."

Herbert, who had forgotten his slight injury, looked down at his discolored hand and gave a laugh.

"Oh, that's nothing," he cried; "if you will get me a little hot water and a bandage, I think we can straighten that out in short order."

She proceeded to do this, bustling about with much intelligence and vivacity. The wound was dressed and she was in the act of binding it up when Mr. and Mrs. Black returned. They were amazed to see Herbert Harkins there, and still more thunderstruck when they learned the story of the attempted robbery. John Black was grateful, but he shook his head as he said to Herbert:

"You should not have released the man. He is a menace to society, and may attempt the same crime against other citizens."

Mary spoke up at this point, saying:

"I disagree with you, father. Herbert was right. He might have been mistaken, but he was merciful and that after all means much in this unfeeling world."

Herbert was delighted at such praise, and bidding her good-night stooped down and kissed her hand in the chivalrous manner of a gentleman of the old school.

The act appeared to please the girl, for her face crimsoned and stooping down, she picked up his wounded hand and gave it a kiss.

"You deserve it," she said impulsively, "because you have acted the part of a hero."

CHAPTER XXIII
IN WHICH A BAD MAN REACHES THE END OF HIS ROPE

Herbert walked home from the Black residence that night. He did not care to ride. He wanted to have the opportunity to think over the exciting incidents of the last hour, and felt that he could not do so with any satisfaction to himself unless he was alone. The clocks were striking one o'clock in the morning when he finally reached his lodgings. The gas was burning in the little sitting room, and Tomlin was there in an attitude of expectancy.

"Well?" he said, with a questioning look. "What was the result of your adventure?"

Herbert's jaw fell. It suddenly dawned upon him that he was once more placed in the attitude of a delinquent. He had unconsciously forgotten all about Tomlin and the fact that he was supposed to be out on an assignment. The thought mortified him very much. He looked into Tomlin's clear eyes, and what he saw there prompted him to be candid. There was no use in attempting to beat about the bush; he would tell the truth and tell it as simply as possible; so he sat down and related all that had occurred from the time he left Tomlin early in the evening until the present moment. Only upon one phase of the story did he attempt any disguise, and that was when he related the threat which had been hurled at him by the burglar. He told his friend that a person who was very dear to Mary Black was in Adler's power, and that the robber had threatened to expose this person and involve him in disgrace if he was not given an immediate release. When Herbert had concluded his narrative, Tomlin leaned back in his chair and gave vent to a hearty laugh. Herbert could not understand the cause of his mirth, and said so. Tomlin laughed again, and then said:

"I don't suppose you see the humorous side of this thing; but it appeals to me very strongly. See here, Harkins, this thing is becoming marked with you. It begins to look as if you had gotten into the habit of falling down on all of your assignments."

"I do feel a bit silly about this," began Herbert, "but you see the position I was placed in. You see it was this way—"

"No explanations are necessary," interrupted Tomlin in his familiar, hearty tones, "explanations are not of much use anyhow. Your friends don't expect them, and your enemies wouldn't believe them. I'm frank to say, however, that you did just what any man with red blood in his veins would have done under the circumstances. In fact I would have acted just as you did."

"Then you don't feel badly over it? You don't blame me—"

"Not at all," interrupted his friend once more; "I only ask you to promise me that you are through with this chivalrous business, and that if you intend to stay in the newspaper profession, you will quit it right here and now, and that hereafter when you are sent out on an assignment you will cover it and write it like a sensible man. Do you promise, Herbert?"

"I promise," said the other meekly.

Thus ended the episode of the attempted robbery. Two days later Herbert started out early in the morning in order to make a tour of the hospitals for the purpose of finding some material for special articles. The first institution he visited was the Samaritan Hospital, with whose superintendent he was on terms of intimacy.

"Got anything to-day?" he said to that official.

"Not much," was the yawning reply, "at least not much out of the ordinary. I don't think we've anything here that you would care for."

"Any deaths to-day?"

"No; but we have a queer sort of fellow here who was shot last night while trying to break into a house up-town."

"Is that so?" remarked Herbert carelessly. "I don't suppose there's anything unusual in the case?"

"No, I don't think so," was the rejoinder. "Here's his name," and the superintendent pushed the big register over in the direction of Herbert.

The young man looked at the open page carelessly, and then gave a sudden start.

The name on the book was decidedly familiar. It was that of Harry Adler. Instantly he became all attention.

"Was the man seriously injured?" he asked anxiously, turning to the superintendent.

"I'm afraid he was; he was shot in the groin while attempting to escape from the house."

"How is he getting along?"

"Badly," was the response; "in fact I am satisfied in my own mind that he is going to make a die of it."

Herbert's sympathies were instantly aroused. He had no regard whatever for Adler, and looked upon him as a very undesirable member of society; but the thought of any man being shot and dying from his wounds appealed strongly to his sympathetic nature.

"I used to know this man at one time," he said; "I wonder if I could be of any use to him. I wonder if he has any friends or relatives that he would care to see."

"I don't know," replied the other.

"Could I see him?" persisted Herbert eagerly; "I might be able to do something."

"Yes," was the ready rejoinder, "come with me."

The two men walked up a flight of stairs and into the accident ward of the hospital. They passed along through row after row of white counterpaned cots. Men of all kinds and descriptions were on these beds of suffering; some within the shadow of the Valley of Death, and others convalescent. In the last cot on the very end row they found the wounded burglar. He presented a pitiable spectacle; and when Herbert looked at his white face and at the countenance twisted with suffering, his heart melted and he forgot all the evil the man had done during his useless life. He groaned with the pain and looked up just as they reached his bedside. His eyes flashed a glance of recognition at Herbert. He put a thin hand outside of the coverlet, and exclaimed eagerly, but in a weak and husky voice:

"Hello there, boy! You're just the person I want to see."

"What is it?" asked Herbert, stooping down and speaking in a gentle voice.

"It's just this," replied the other in a voice that was not more than audible; "I am satisfied that I've reached the end of my rope. The doctor says there's no hope for me. I suppose it serves me right, but that don't make me feel any better. I know I've led a very miserable existence, and I suppose that as a man lives so he must die. It's too late for me to do any good in the world now; but while I have the strength and the voice I'd like to clear up one little thing in which I am satisfied you have a personal interest."

"Yes?" assented Herbert with much eagerness, bending a little lower so that he might hear the man's voice; "what is it about?"

"It's about the robbery of John Black's house in Cleverly."

"I thought so," exclaimed Herbert, his eyes sparkling with the excitement of the moment; "what is it you want to tell me?"

"Well," said the other, "you know all about the rumors that flew around Cleverly at that time. Your father's name was involved. I want to tell you, and it's a dying man who is speaking to you, that he was innocent of that."

"I know it," replied Herbert; "but who was guilty?"

"I'll tell you that very briefly," answered the stricken man. "You know the kind of fellow I was. I had no scruples. I wanted to live without work. I got acquainted with young Arthur Black, and I am afraid that I was the means of corrupting his morals. I traveled with him a great deal, and he learned many vicious habits through me. Well, this went on for some time, and one day I was filled with the desire of getting a good stake and running off to New York. In the course of my acquaintance with Arthur Black I learned that his father sometimes brought home money from the bank. On this particular day a customer who came in from the country late in the afternoon was anxious to make a deposit. It was after business hours, and the safe had been closed and locked for the day. The cashier, who was charged with the care of the vault, had gone home and could not be reached. To accommodate the depositor, Mr. Black accepted his money and took it home with him that night. I was hanging around the door of the bank at this time and overheard the conversation between the two men. I was tempted. It isn't necessary to say that it did not take much to tempt me; but I was filled with an unquenchable desire to get hold of that money.

"Well," continued the wounded man, his voice becoming lower and lower, "I hunted up Arthur immediately and managed to spend the next two hours with him. I pumped him about the habits of his father and the routine of their household. I wanted to know particularly how he was able to get in the house when he left me late at night as he often did. He said, in his innocence, that his mother was always his friend, and that in spite of the anger of his father she persisted in taking care of him. One of the ways she employed to do this was to leave the key of the dead latch of the door under the mat which lay on the front porch. That was the very thing I was anxious to learn, and when I discovered it I left Arthur abruptly, saying that I would see him the next night. It was after midnight when I went around to the Black house. The inmates apparently were asleep. I hung around till nearly one o'clock in the morning, anxious that all the conditions should be ripe for my dishonest enterprise. When I lifted the mat I found the key there as it had been described to me by Arthur Black. I got into the house without difficulty and went to the old man's desk. It was one of those frail roll-top affairs, and I succeeded in breaking into it without any difficulty. I took the money, and then to throw them off the scent, broke the bolt on the back door to convey the impression that the robber had entered in that manner."

"What happened then?" asked Herbert eagerly.

"The rest is soon told," said Adler, his voice sinking to the merest whisper; "I became aware of the excitement that had been created by the robbery and kept myself in seclusion for some days. I felt a little bad when I learned that an effort had been made to place the robbery on your father, and when he died I was almost on the verge of making a confession; but didn't do it. Some days after this I decided to go to New York with the money, and in a fit of devilishness resolved to take Arthur Black to New York with me. It seemed to me a very clever trick to entertain this foolish boy with the money that I had stolen from his father. You know the rest. We came here and he went from bad to worse until we got into that get-rich-quick concern which led to the breaking up of our partnership. Something happened to him then. What it was I have never discovered; but the boy turned good, and left me, saying that our paths would lie in different directions in the future; and he has kept his word from that day to this. You remember what happened the other night when you had me cornered in old Black's house. I used Arthur's name to secure my own liberty. There you have the whole story. I'm sorry for what I've done; that's all I can say."

The importance of this confession was appreciated by Herbert, who through the assistance of the superintendent, hastily summoned a stenographer and a Notary Public. Although the effort was a very painful one, Adler repeated his story just as he had told it to Herbert. After it had been reduced to writing, he swore to the truth of it, and then having a pen placed within his trembling fingers, signed his name in scrawling lines.

Herbert asked the man if there was anything he could do for him. He said if it was possible to lighten his last hours in any way he would be only too glad to do it; but Adler shook his head in a melancholy way and said he had no request to make. Herbert wanted to know if he had relatives or friends he wished to see before his death. Once more he shook his head, and added:

"My mother died when I was only a few years old; my father never took care of me. I don't know now whether he is dead or alive, and even if I was aware of his abiding place I would not ask him to come here."

Herbert felt a strange lump coming into his throat at these words. He wondered with a queer feeling about his heart whether he would have been any better than this dying man if his early life and surroundings had been the same; but when he left the hospital it was with a feeling of elation over the strange manner in which every detail of the Cleverly mystery had been brought to light. The vindication of his father's memory was absolutely complete, and he could now go out into the world with a firm step and with his head in the air. On his return to his room he told the whole story to Tomlin, who listened with absorbed attention. Late that afternoon he made another call at the Samaritan Hospital. The superintendent, who was in the office, gave him a nod of recognition.

"How is that wounded man?" asked Herbert.

"Dead," was the terse reply.

CHAPTER XXIV
WHEREIN THE CLOUDS PASS AWAY AND THE SUN SHINES ON HERBERT HARKINS

Herbert Harkins voluntarily assumed the care and disposal of the remains of the unfortunate criminal. The young reporter was acquainted with the Coroner's undertaker and through his assistance and that of some mutual friends he was able to secure a cheap lot in an out of town cemetery. The obsequies of the departed one were pathetic in the extreme. The only two mourners at the funeral—if they could be called mourners—were Herbert Harkins and Francis Tomlin. The whole affair was tinged with an atmosphere that was at once sombre and desolate; but at all events Adler had been given a Christian burial, and that was the thing that Herbert desired most of all.

"You're a curious fellow, Harkins," said Tomlin to the young man on their way home from the cemetery.

"How do you make that out?" asked Herbert.

"Why, by your actions," was the reply; "you are constantly doing unexplainable things. Take to-day for instance. Who else would have done so much for a man who was the cause of all his troubles?"

"Ah!" said Herbert, "but you must understand that my troubles are now buried in the grave with that poor, miserable man. I can afford to be generous."

"Even if you are not just?"

"Who shall determine that—I for one shall always shrink from being the judge of my fellow men."

"But you know that this Adler was thoroughly disreputable—"

"Yes," interrupted Herbert, "and that is all the more reason why I should be reputable. A man must be merciful if he looks for mercy himself."

They had reached their rooms by this time, and after a few preliminaries, Herbert sat down at his desk and began to clear up an accumulation of work that had been neglected during the past week, largely because his time was taken up in preparing for the funeral arrangements of Harry Adler. This work occupied his attention almost constantly till late in the night. His last act was to write a letter to his mother at Cleverly, reminding her that she would be expected to arrive in New York on Christmas Eve, which important occasion would occur on the following day. He put a special delivery stamp on the letter and carried it around to one of the sub-post office stations in order to insure its prompt delivery on the following morning.

When the day before Christmas arrived it brought with it a fine fall of snow, and quite early in the morning the face of New York was hidden from view with a soft, fleecy covering. At noon time that day Herbert received a telegram from his mother saying that she would be unable to reach New York till about eleven o'clock on Christmas morning. It seemed odd that she should disappoint him in this unaccountable way; but he thrust the telegram in his pocket, and in the rush of his everyday duties quickly forgot the incident.

That evening Tomlin came into the house with a rather solemn face and said to Herbert:

"I have been made the bearer of a message to you. Mr. Blakeley says that he would like to see you at the Argus office at nine o'clock this evening."

Herbert's face flushed at this unexpected announcement. It was the first time that he had heard from Blakeley either directly or indirectly, since the dramatic incident which terminated his career on the newspaper. At first the message filled him with a sense of elation; but this was quickly followed by a feeling of resentment. His face hardened, and he said with much dignity:

"If Mr. Blakeley desires to communicate with me, or to call upon me, he knows my address. I—"

"Now see here," quickly interrupted Tomlin, "I don't want any of this nonsense from you. I don't care what you do or what you say to Blakeley; but I don't propose to have you make me look silly and ridiculous."

Herbert melted in a minute. The distress and annoyance in his friend's face changed his whole manner.

"I wouldn't offend you for a moment, Tomlin," he said; "you have been such a good friend to me that there isn't anything in the world that I would not do to serve you. I had felt a bit angry towards Blakeley, but I could not hold anything but the kindest feelings toward you. If you say go, I'll go in a minute."

Tomlin's answer was clear, crisp and to the point. He simply said in his loudest voice:

"Go!"

At nine o'clock that evening Herbert found himself ascending the stairway toward the local room of the Argus. When he entered, a number of the men were busily engaged at their desks; but they all looked up and gave him a cheery greeting. The old familiar scenes coming upon him unexpectedly seemed to rush through his memory like floods of water surging over a falls. Blakeley, as usual, occupied his desk in the corner of the room. He looked quite lifelike to Herbert as he sat there puffing a strong cigar, with his feet cocked up on the edge of his desk, reading a proof that had just been rushed down from the composing room.

The moment he perceived Herbert he moved his feet from the desk, arose from his chair, and extending his hand, said with considerable cordiality:

"Hello, Harkins, I'm glad to see you again."

Herbert took the proffered hand, but held it somewhat limply. He could not enthuse on such short notice. Presently he was invited to take a seat, and did so. Tomlin, without being asked, also sat down to listen to the conversation.

"I was quite sorry to lose you, Harkins," said Blakeley after an interval.

Herbert looked in his face for a moment to see whether he was jesting. Such an admission from such a man was very unusual; but Blakeley looked him squarely in the eye, and there was neither mirth nor sarcasm in the glance, so he answered softly:

"I was sorry to go, Mr. Blakeley."

"But," exclaimed the city editor, and the quiet eye now flashed fire, "you treated me very meanly. I must say that, and I am going to repeat it, you treated me very meanly."

"I admit that I did," said Herbert, his tone softer than before; "but I was the victim of circumstances over which I had no control."

Blakeley puffed at his cigar for awhile after that, and then as if he was giving voice to a long cherished desire, said:

"Now see here, Harkins, I want to put a plain question to you. Why did you refuse to write that story—now tell me as plainly as you can, and all will be square between us."

Herbert arose before the city editor had finished making his request. The look of annoyance in his face gave way to indignation, and then he said with considerable heat:

"Is that all you have to say to me, Mr. Blakeley?" and receiving no answer, he went on, "If it is, I will leave you. There is no need of any further conversation between us."

At this point Blakeley arose with a smile on his face that seemed to stretch almost from ear to ear. His eyes were sparkling with good nature, and going over to Herbert he took his hand and wrung it heartily.

"You are all right, my boy; you are pure gold. I don't propose to let you get out of here again. I need you in my business."

Herbert was plainly puzzled at this demonstration, and said so at once.

"I don't know why you should be so pleased, Mr. Blakeley. I have declined to answer your query."

"That's just it," he said; "it demonstrates what I have always believed, that you wouldn't betray a confidence. However a kind friend has already done that for you."

Herbert's eyes expressed the surprise he felt. Before he could make any reply a door in the rear of Mr. Blakeley's office opened suddenly, and Arthur Black appeared upon the scene. Herbert gasped for breath. He was too much amazed to speak to the young man. Blakeley spared him that trouble by saying:

"Now, Mr. Black, we are all together; tell me once again the story that you were good enough to relate to me early in the afternoon."

"The story is soon told," said Arthur, with a firmness in his voice and a dignity in his manner that Herbert had never noticed before; "I come here to do a tardy act of justice to one of the manliest persons I have ever known. Mr. Blakeley, as I have already told you, I was foolish enough and despicable enough to engage in, or rather to permit myself to be used in a swindling game that was being conducted in this city some time ago. Herbert Harkins ran that story out for the Argus and was prepared to make an arrest of one of those who were engaged in the game; but when he discovered that I was implicated in it he permitted me to escape, and as a result of that act of generosity, lost a good story and forfeited his position on the Argus.

"I left the city immediately after that incident occurred," continued Arthur, "and went to a little town in Connecticut, where I endeavored to make a new man of myself. I think I have partially succeeded. I am not going to stop till I succeed entirely; but only a week ago I learned of the misfortune which had happened to Herbert Harkins through his effort to shield me and my family from disgrace. I have not been able to rest at night since I learned this news. Finally I could stand it no longer, and I came here to tell you the truth and the simple truth. Herbert did throw the Argus down on its good story, but he did so for my sake and the sake of my father and mother and sister. I am here now not only to admit this, but to throw myself on your mercy. If you think the ends of justice have not already been served, I am willing to submit to arrest and imprisonment. The punishment will be a severe one, but probably not more than I deserve. In any event I hope to restore Herbert

Harkins to your esteem, if not to the position he formerly occupied on this paper."

Herbert listened to this recital in open mouthed wonder. He watched Arthur Black keenly while he was telling his story, and as he proceeded, was filled with admiration for the young man. He could see very clearly now that Arthur was not really a bad boy at heart; that he had been a spoiled child in his youth and had drifted into the company of dissolute young men. What at first was merely waywardness had gradually extended to more serious things; but fortunately his downward career had been checked just on the edge of a precipice.

There was silence in the group for a few moments, and then Blakeley spoke up in his short, snappy tones. He took Arthur by the hand, and said:

"I want to congratulate you, young man. You have shown a manliness that does you credit. Now, there is no paper in town that is more eager to obtain exclusive news than the Argus, and I am willing to admit that there are times when we feel disposed to turn sharp corners in order to beat the other newspapers; but we have the line of decency even in this office, and I propose to draw it on this occasion. You can rest at your ease. So far as I am concerned and so far as the paper is concerned, the firm with which you were connected never existed; the incident at the post office never happened. I can only say that you have my best wishes for your future success in life."

Everybody was delighted at this evidence of a warm heart on the part of the man who had the reputation of being a cold-blooded hunter for news. But he was not through. He turned to Herbert after a few moments of meditation, and said:

"Harkins, your old place awaits you on the Argus. I want to tell you, as I have already told young Black, that my memory is a blank, that you have never offended me and that you have never thrown the paper down. Your place has never been filled. Your chair over at that desk is still vacant. Come in again on Monday morning and try to distinguish yourself."

The manner of this man, no less than the words, impressed Herbert deeply, and he mentally vowed that he would do his duty by Blakeley and the Argus to the full extent of his ability.

There was much laughter and much hand shaking as the little party dispersed. Tomlin lingered a little longer than the others, and when they were out of ear-shot, said to Blakeley in quick tones:

"Say, old man, that was a cruel test with which you began this session—that attempt to get Herbert to squeal on Arthur Black."

"Aye," responded the other heartily, "it was indeed, but it was the crucial test. It was worth all the pain that it cost. It is proof positive to my mind that Harkins can be trusted absolutely. He would die before he violated a confidence. That's the kind of men we need on the Argus."

CHAPTER XXV
DEMONSTRATING THE TRUTH OF THE SAYING THAT ALL'S WELL THAT ENDS WELL

Christmas morning dawned cold and clear and crisp with a nipping eagerness in the atmosphere that brought the roses to the cheeks and warmed the hearts of the multitudes who made their abode on Manhattan Island. The spirit of the day seemed to take hold of everybody and manifested itself in the homes of the lowly as well as in those of the great. Herbert attended early morning Mass, and as he knelt before the crib of the Infant Saviour of the world, his heart swelled with a feeling of profound gratefulness for all the graces and favors that had been showered upon him. Nowhere did the meaning of the day seem more apparent than in the little apartment which had been occupied so long by Herbert Harkins and his friend Tomlin.

At ten o'clock that morning Tomlin turned to Herbert and said:

"See here, old man, if you don't hurry to the railroad station you are likely to miss your mother."

"Why, what's the matter with you, Tomlin? You're as nervous and fidgety as an old cat. The train doesn't come in for an hour yet."

"Yes, yes, I know," said Tomlin in hurried tones. "But you can't depend on these New York trains. They're always ahead of time. Suppose your mother got in and was waiting there now."

"Why," exclaimed the other, with a skeptical look in his face, "I thought the trains were generally behind time."

"No, no," responded the other in his nervous, jerky way. "Ahead of time; ahead of time, always! But see here, don't you stand there trying to get into an argument with me. You go and fetch your mother. She has never been in New York. Suppose she should start to come here herself and get lost—and lost on Christmas morning, too. Why, the idea is too terrible to contemplate."

Herbert departed in a few minutes, much to the satisfaction of his friend. The understanding was that he should bring his mother to their little abode, and then after the arrangement of some preliminaries, that the three should go to a well known restaurant for their holiday dinner. The moment Herbert disappeared, however, there were strange doings in that neighborhood. Tomlin stepped to the front door and gave a low whistle. Immediately two men stepped from within the shadows of friendly doorways and joined him. One was Horace Coke and the other Noah Brooks, who had hurried up from Cleverly in order to join in the conspiracy that had been laid by Francis Tomlin.

"Now, boys!" shouted the youth to the two elderly men; "get down to work as soon as you can."

And they did. A bag filled with holly and evergreen appeared as if by magic. Each of them grabbed a handful, and in an incredibly short space of time the doorways and windows and the gas fixtures were artistically draped. After this the little extension table was drawn out and filled with all the additional leaves that it would hold. Then a long tablecloth that had been engaged for the occasion was thrown over the table. It was as white and as pure as the driven snow, and even without any food was an incentive to good cheer. In the meantime a boy from a neighboring store appeared with eight or ten additional chairs, carrying them one at a time into the little apartment.

"It's going to be a tight squeeze," said Tomlin, "but I think we'll make it."

"Oh, yes," exclaimed Brooks, "it's going to be tight all right; but the more the merrier is always my motto."

While the three conspirators were talking, John Black and his wife and Mary Black appeared as if by appointment. Mary insisted upon joining in the housework, and her deft little fingers rapidly completed the details that had not already been attended to. John Anderson, the school teacher, who had placed Herbert on the path which led to ultimate success, dropped in a little later, and to cap the climax, who should hove into view but Captain Thomas Janson, bluff and hearty and loud-mouthed as ever. He sailed into the room like a whiff of salt air, and his mere presence was refreshing and invigorating. He was handsomely attired for the occasion. He had discarded his ordinary clothing, and wore a handsome blue suit, with brass buttons and gilt stripes on the sleeves, giving him, as one of the other guests slyly remarked, the appearance of a Rear Admiral of the United States Navy. A nautical cap sat jauntily on the Captain's shock of bushy red hair. He puffed like a porpoise, for he was quite stout now and beginning to feel the effects of age. When he had finally settled himself comfortably in a large chair which had been placed for him at the head of the table, he turned around to the others and cried out in his loudest voice:

"Does the boy know which way the wind blows?"

"No!" came a chorus in reply.

"Good!" he exclaimed; "then it will fall to the lot of old Captain Janson to tell him something about the voyage of life."

Tomlin looked at his watch at this period. It pointed to high noon. He turned to the Captain:

"Herbert will be here in fifteen or twenty minutes. I guess we had better start. What do you say?"

"Sure," snorted the old salt.

Without waiting for any further remarks, Tomlin charged out of the front door, and in a few minutes returned, followed by two white aproned and white capped fellows, carrying waiters which contained plates filled with eatables that were smoking hot. When the covers were removed the air was impregnated with an appetizing odor. The two mates, as the Captain insisted upon calling the two waiters, made five or six trips before they finally completed their work to their satisfaction and declared everything all right.

And indeed it was all right. The table presented a beautiful sight, charming to the eye and tempting to the palate. An enormous turkey, browned to a crisp, occupied the center of the table; mounds of mashed white potatoes and roasted sweet potatoes, and dishes of cranberries moulded into the most incomprehensible shapes—all looked so clean and sweet that they must have tempted the most jaded appetite. A row of mince pies flanked on either side by delicious looking pumpkin pies, suggested that the diners were expected to do some very serious work before their day's labor was finished.

"Now all hands be seated," cried the Captain; "but don't dare to eat a mouthful until I give the signal."

He had scarcely finished this caution when the door opened, and Herbert entered, accompanied by his mother; and then there were such cheers and shouts and such laughter and such crying as had never been heard before in this old room since its first walls had been constructed.

Herbert was literally made speechless by amazement. His mother, with feminine instinct, took refuge in tears; but Herbert soon recovered his voice and his mother soon dried her tears, and very quickly the clatter of knives and forks and the din of conversation and the ripple of never-ending laughter set everyone at ease.

Tomlin, in a spirit of mischief, had set Herbert Harkins and Mary Black side by side, and during the dinner the two young people were made the subject of many good natured jests; but Mary's sweet countenance glowed with happiness, and when Herbert stooped down to speak to her once during the dinner her cheeks crimsoned in the most beautiful manner imaginable.

Some philosopher—if he wasn't a philosopher he should have been one— has said that it never rains but it pours. So it was on this festive occasion. The first shower came with the announcement that within six months Herbert would be given the coveted post of Washington correspondent of the Argus—that he should join the company of the very aristocracy of

American journalism. The next came with the statement that Blakeley—good-hearted, blustering Blakeley—had been made the managing editor of the Argus, and that Tomlin would succeed him in the responsible position of city editor of that journal. At this announcement Herbert seized the hand of his friend and wrung it with such fervor that his old room-mate cried for mercy. After that John Black informed the assembled company of the selection of his son Arthur as the cashier and confidential man of his newly established bank at Cleverly.

Captain Janson was given the floor then, and amid many elaborate sea phrases and involved sentences he proclaimed Herbert Harkins as his adopted son and heir.

Near the close of the dinner, Herbert arose and with trembling lips and swelling heart announced that the noblest girl in the whole world had just promised to become his wife; and although he mentioned no name, every eye turned instinctively towards Mary, who finding herself singled out from all the others, blushed desperately and shrank shyly beneath the united gaze of the company for all the world like a sweet little violet whose hiding place has been discovered by a sudden burst of glaring sunlight.

Milton Keynes UK
Ingram Content Group UK Ltd.
UKHW010852010724
444982UK00005B/550